6.95

FIRST
SERVE

Mary Towne

FIRST SERVE

DRAWINGS BY

RUTH SANDERSON

Atheneum • *New York*

1976

Library of Congress Cataloging in Publication Data
Towne, Mary. First serve.
SUMMARY: Relates the events of a crucial summer during
which a talented thirteen-year-old tennis player must
make a commitment not only to her tennis career but to
herself as an individual.
[1. Tennis—Fiction.   2. Family life—Fiction]
I. Sanderson, Ruth.   II. Title.
PZ7.T6495Fi   [Fic]   76-100
ISBN 0-689-30532-X

Published simultaneously in Canada by
McClelland & Stewart, Ltd.
Manufactured in the United States of America by
Halliday Lithograph Corporation
West Hanover, Massachusetts
Designed by Mary M. Ahern
First Edition

FIRST
SERVE

one

OUR FAMILY goes to Forest Hills almost every September to see the tennis, usually during the week before the finals. The tickets are cheaper then, and you have a choice of matches to watch. Sometimes the tennis in the early rounds turns out to be a lot more exciting than the finals, anyway. That year, the fall of 1974, we were going on the Thursday, and taking my little brother Eric along for the first time.

"Good," said Mrs. Trask, when I mentioned it to her. "It's about time you sat back and enjoyed somebody else's tennis for a change. Maybe you'll get to see some of the good women players, if all this rain hasn't delayed the schedule too much. You've been before, haven't you?"

"Oh, yes. But this year . . ." I hesitated, playing with the zipper of my racket cover. There were still times when I felt shy with Mrs. Trask. "Well, this year is different, I guess."

"Meaning this year you're not just going along for the ride?" She smiled. "Well, take a good look around, Dulcie. Who knows, maybe someday you won't need a ticket for Forest Hills."

I didn't know about that, but I did know how much everything had changed for me over the weeks of that summer. The summer before last. . . . A lot has happened since, but that's really what I want to tell you about: how that summer began, and how it ended.

But first I want to think about our day at Forest Hills while it's still sharp and clear in my mind; but distant, too, like a picture seen through binoculars. Because it was the following weekend that everything changed for me once more—when I was brought face-to-face, at last, with the thing I'd been trying to evade all my life. There were no protective lenses then, for any of us.

AS MY FATHER SAYS, there may be plenty of tennis courts in Forest Hills, but there aren't any forests, hills, or places to park. The special little parking lot he remembered from our last visit had either vanished or become the site of an apartment building. Anyway, we never found it, and by the time we'd dumped the car on a side street somewhere (Mom was sure we'd never see it again) and walked several blocks to the stadium, the first match of the day had already begun. Dad said it was going to be a long afternoon of tennis anyhow, so it didn't matter if we missed a set or two. None of us really agreed with this, except maybe Eric, but nobody said anything.

But at last we were sitting in our places, squashed together on a hard bench high above the three stadium courts—the five members of the Kane family in the midst of about ten thousand other people. Down on the grass, Ken Rosewall, in a yellow shirt and white shorts, was leading in his match against the young Indian player Vijay Amritraj (white shirt, white shorts) in the quarter-finals of the 1974 U.S. Open.

It was a brilliant blue September day, breezy around the edges, and the sun shone hot on our faces. I knew my father would have a sunburned nose by the end of the day, and would tell me to go find the Solarcaine for him; in our family, I'm the one who finds things. My mother was wearing one of those white paper sun shields they supply there and was mad at herself for forgetting to bring a hat. "I have to go to work tomorrow, after all," she said. "*I* can't afford to get sunstroke like the rest of you free-loaders."

Which was hardly fair to my father, who was taking his annual two-week vacation from the store

—all he ever allows himself, even in good times— and who works long hours the rest of the year. But he just laughed and told my mother she was too hard-headed ever to get sunstroke. "You're solid gold, sweetie," he added when she looked offended, and patted the top of her Clairol-blonde head; and she had to smile in spite of herself.

The crowd groaned as Amritraj put an easy volley into the net and walked back to the baseline, shaking his head dejectedly.

"What's the matter with the kid, anyway?" my father grumbled. "After that terrific match he played against Borg . . ."

My older sister Pat said, "He's just not moving. He needs to get up to the net sooner."

I said, "He looks kind of psyched out. It's funny, because he plays the same kind of game as Rosewall, in a way. But maybe that makes it harder—Rosewall being so much more experienced." The tension, I meant, and the huge crowd, and how if your game depends more on speed and accuracy than on power, you have to keep your cool no matter what.

But whatever else I might have said—and I was talking out of turn, anyway, in our family it was Pat who was supposed to know about tennis—was forgotten in a great roar of excitement from the crowd. Amritraj had come up fast on his serve for a change and had managed to get his racket solidly on Rosewall's backhand return. He volleyed it perfectly down the line for what looked like a winner—except that Rosewall was there somehow, streaking along the baseline in time to send a high lob over the Indian player's head. The ball was falling short, though; and I waited for Amritraj to smash it for a sure putaway (if anything's ever sure against Rosewall). Instead he chose to let the ball bounce, and hit a drop shot, a little dink that just cleared the net.

It was a risky thing to do, but it should have worked; and we all gasped as Rosewall came up on the dead run, skidded down onto one knee, and flicked up another desperation lob. This time Amritraj did hit the overhead—and hit it out, a good two feet beyond the baseline.

"Wow!"

We were all laughing, the thing was so fantastic.

"Well," Dad said, "I guess that proves it's always worth getting the ball back, even when it looks like you've had it."

Just what Mrs. Trask was always telling me: run out every ball, Dulcie, no matter how hopeless it seems. But I didn't say anything. No one else knew about Mrs. Trask, not really. No one knew about my crazy dream that sometimes didn't seem like a dream at all but a certainty—a matter of hard work and time and maybe a few breaks along the way. Pat was still our tennis player, the main reason we were all here at Forest Hills—playing hooky in fact, except for Dad, since school had started yesterday, and even Mom was taking the day off from her job.

My little brother was pounding me on the knee. "I want a hot dog, Dulcie. You said I could have a hot dog!"

"I did not, Eric. We brought our own lunch, and we're not going to spend money on a lot of other junk. Here." I bent double, trying to drag the picnic basket out from under my seat—we really were crammed together on that bench. "I made you a baloney sandwich with lots of mustard, the way you like it. And there's egg too, and liverwurst, and— let's see—ham and cheese—"

"I want a hot dog," Eric insisted.

"*Ssh!*" I said, as the man in front of us turned around, looking irritated. He didn't say anything, though. Tennis fans are still pretty polite, even if Billie Jean King says they shouldn't be. Amritraj had lost his serve, the players had changed sides, and a new game was beginning.

Eric squirmed in his seat beside me, jogging my arm so that I almost dropped the thermos of milk I was trying to open.

"Well, this is boring," he complained. "You can hardly even *see* them."

Not like on TV, he meant. He'd had the same disappointment at a baseball game we'd gone to that spring—no close-ups of the batter, no instant replays.

I said, "But Eric, this is real! I mean, we're here,

and it's happening here, right now! Half the stuff you see on TV is on tape, anyhow."

But this argument didn't impress him. He refused the baloney sandwich and went on begging for a hot dog. Meanwhile I poured milk and passed out sandwiches and missed a spectacular exchange of volleys down on the court that had everyone around me standing and applauding.

"Oh, nuts," my father said at last. "Go get Eric a hot dog, will you, Dulcie? Maybe that'll calm him down."

I looked from my half-eaten sandwich to the pale grass of the Forest Hills courts below, scuffed up along the baselines and showing bare patches from ten days of tournament play, not at all lush and manicured the way you might expect—but still, as I'd told Eric, the place where it was happening.

I said, "I will when this match is over."

"Amritraj has had it, anyway. Down two sets and behind in this one—"

"He won the first one," I said stubbornly. "Maybe he can get something going again."

It was true that the young Indian looked rather dispirited now, his shoulders drooping in the moments between points. But as he waited to receive Rosewall's serve, he went into a tense half-crouch, his head came up, his whole body expressed his willingness to make the best of whatever was going to happen next, win or lose. And that's sportsmanship,

I thought. Maybe Billie Jean is right. Never mind about being little ladies and gentlemen on the tennis court who never talk to themselves or throw their rackets or yell at linesmen—the real thing is built into the game itself, and it doesn't have anything to do with country club manners.

But I smiled to myself, imagining what Mrs. Trask would say if she ever caught me throwing my racket.

Dad said impatiently, "Oh, come on, Dulcie, you're not going to miss anything."

"Eric can go get his own hot dog, if he wants one so much."

I kept my eyes on the court, but I could feel my father looking at me in surprise. Why was I being so uncooperative, all of a sudden? After all, I'd been to Forest Hills before.

"No I can't," Eric was protesting. "I don't know where to go!"

I said, "Yes, you can, Eric. It's just down those stairs; there's a refreshment stand right there."

"Well, I don't know." My father looked worried. "I don't want him getting lost in this mob—"

"Oh, Dad! Eric's seven years old, for heaven's sake!"

"Hey!" Pat leaned over from her seat beyond my mother. "Cool it down there, can't you?"

She turned back to the game, her profile serious and intent. You couldn't see the scar, it was on the other side.

10

"Oh, well." Dad stood up. "I feel like stretching my legs, anyhow. Whoever numbered these seats must have been expecting a bunch of midgets. Come on, sport, I'll buy you your hot dog."

He and Eric bumped their way past people's knees over to the aisle and disappeared around the stairway portal.

Peace, I thought. And space. . . . I tried to relax on the hard bench and concentrate on the tennis. But Pat's words rankled in a way she hadn't intended. Cool it! Oh sure, easy enough for her to say. She wasn't the one who'd fixed breakfast and cleaned up afterwards and made sandwiches and kept Eric amused in the car on the way in from Connecticut. All of that was my department. Ordinarily I didn't mind, but today I felt irritable and out of sorts. So much for sitting back and enjoying the tennis, I thought glumly.

Pat's department was—well, being talented and succeeding at things, I guess. She had her tennis in the summer and her art and music and math in the winter, and that seemed to be enough for Mom and Dad. Pat complained about how our parents spoiled Eric, but maybe hers was a kind of spoiling too. But I was instantly ashamed of the thought. After all, I knew why they felt the way they did. Sometimes I thought they were wrong, but I couldn't really blame them.

As for me—pretty Dulcie, she's only thirteen, but already the boys are hanging around; a good student, not brilliant like Pat, but she works hard. Oh, we never worry about Dulcie, she's so responsible —and such a help around the house, I don't know what I'd do without her. . . . Well, I guess everybody overhears their mother's telephone conversations from time to time without meaning to, or even particularly wanting to. And up until this last summer, I'd never really objected to any of it, except for my name.

Dulcie! I know what it means: gentle and sweet, like *dolce* in music. Pat and I had a good laugh over that one, the first time she came across it in one of her piano pieces. At least Pat knows me better than that.

I told Mrs. Trask once how I felt about it, saying why couldn't I have had a nice simple name like Sue or Ann, and she smiled and said, "But Dulcie's such a *pretty* name! And you look so pretty on the court, too—as if maybe all you were going to do was model tennis dresses out there. . . ."

She shook her head sadly. "Just think what a terrible shock it's going to be when you start rushing the net and slamming volleys around and hanging onto every set point like some ugly old bulldog. Disguise is a big part of tennis, you know, Dulcie. Think of your name as a kind of secret weapon—your looks too. You'll be getting into the finals before anyone knows what's hit them."

Well, maybe. No, not maybe; for sure. Think

sure, as Mrs. Trask kept telling me whenever I had to make a difficult shot. I clenched my left hand—that's another weapon of sorts, my being left-handed—and let it relax and began paying attention again to the here-and-now tennis, especially Rosewall's famous left-handed backhand.

After a while Dad and Eric came back, Rosewall took the set 6–2 for the match, and Stan Smith came out to warm up with Roscoe Tanner, a young, unseeded player with a big serve, or so we'd heard.

Mom leaned over and nudged me. "Hey, how about this Tanner boy, Dulcie? A real dreamboat!" She has this awful old slang she never seems to use with anyone but me.

Hoping nobody around us had heard, I shrugged. "If you like the type."

"Clean-cut," my mother pronounced. "Not drowning in his own hair like that what's-his-name, Borg, that all you kids go for."

"Connors is the one I go for," I said, sharply for me. "As a *player,* Mom." In fact I was looking forward to seeing Connors play later on that afternoon. "I mean, maybe he's conceited and all, like they say, but I think he's got the best all-around game."

She gave me a look. "Since when did you get to be such an expert on tennis, I'd like to know?"

But the match was beginning, and I was saved from answering. Big serve, big volley, big deal. It's not the kind of tennis I enjoy watching for very long, though Tanner did have a nifty passing shot that got the crowd cheering.

Also I was feeling restless and jittery. My mother's remark had reminded me that I was going to have to talk to her and Dad soon about Mrs. Trask's plans for me—if only because we'd be moving to an indoor court for my practice sessions, every day after school if Mrs. Trask had her way. I didn't see how I was going to manage that, even if I could explain it to my parents in the first place. They'd think I'd gone crazy, or that Mrs. Trask had. If only I'd let her call them earlier in the summer, as she'd wanted to do. . . .

But I knew that in the long run it was really up to me.

I said I was tired of sitting and wanted to wander around and see what else was going on. I tried the grandstand, where Newcombe and Ashe were playing their quarter-final match, but the place was packed, and they weren't letting anyone else in. People stood five deep around the fence outside, trying to get a glimpse of the play, with all the tallest men in front, it seemed. I wormed my way forward as far as I could and stood on tiptoe, craning my neck this way and that. I got several head-and-shoulders views of the players as they reached up to serve—Newcombe with his pink shirt and pirate mustache, Ashe in blue, looking calm and unruffled as usual—but I couldn't see any of the game itself. After a while I decided to move on, hoping there might be a good women's match going on on one of the outside courts.

As I turned away, I almost fell over a kid who was down on his knees by the fence of the nearest court, trying to wrestle a tennis ball out through the heavy mesh. He almost had it too, squeezing the ball hard in his grubby fingers, when one of the ball boys inside spotted him and ran over and wrenched it angrily out of his grasp. The kid stood up, shaking his head and grinning, and I grinned back at him. I knew how he felt: a ball from Forest Hills, even just a practice ball, would be a souvenir worth having.

I ambled along the gravel paths between the courts, wondering what it felt like to play on grass, and whether I'd ever have the chance to. I'd heard they were going to replace the grass courts in the stadium here with a composition surface by next year. Well, okay, I'd just have to make it to Wimbledon then. . . .

Aside from a senior men's doubles match, nothing much seemed to be going on, so I had a Coke in the shade of a marquee and started back. I recognized a famous actor and a TV newscaster my parents often watched, but they didn't interest me. Where were the women players I'd come to see? Bad enough that there weren't any women's singles matches scheduled today—I'd thought I might at least see some of the players out practicing, or just wandering around, or . . .

I stopped. On the court next to me, ten feet

away, Virginia Wade was bending over to retrieve a ball. She called something in a high-pitched English voice to the woman on the other side of the net— Lesley Hunt, maybe? I knew they were supposed to play a doubles match later on, if there was time; but we'd be on our way back to Connecticut by then. My father said we couldn't keep Eric up too late.

Virginia Wade straightened up, smiling—she has a marvelous smile—and walked to the baseline to serve. Whenever I'd seen her on TV, she'd looked kind of grim and tense, as if she were fighting herself more than her opponent, and it was fun to see her relaxed and easy, just playing a practice set or two.

I watched intently, storing away impressions to think about later. She wasn't wearing a tennis dress, just a white T-shirt and shorts, and you could see the strength in her shoulders and arms and muscular legs —the athlete's body which, to me anyway, is the most truly feminine of all because it's been developed and *used,* not just draped around for decoration. She seemed shorter than she appears on TV, and it occurred to me that except for Chris Evert and Margaret Court, most of the top women players are on the short side, even kind of chunky in build. I'm short myself—of course I haven't got my full height yet, but I'll probably never be more than five-four or five —so this thought pleased me. Sometimes, watching my sister Pat on the tennis court, I've thought she was just too tall and lanky for the game, without the power or coordination that would make up for her height—or make the most of it, whichever way you look at it.

With Mrs. Trask in mind, I paid particular attention to Wade's serve, which is supposed to be one of the strongest in women's tennis. She wasn't going all out, of course, but still you could see how she really attacked the ball, getting her whole body behind her racket at the moment of impact—and all of it a forward motion, so that she seemed to arrive at the net before the ball even had a chance to bounce on the other side.

Economy, I thought, one of Mrs. Trask's favorite words. No waste motion. I'm naturally quick, and lately she'd been getting me to shorten my backswing, even on deep ground strokes. "I don't want you to chop at the ball, Dulcie," she explained when I tried it. "You've still got to hit your strokes properly, and in rhythm. Just try speeding up the camera a bit." As for my serve—well, it was never going to be anything spectacular, not like Wade's, but as long as it got me to the net. . . .

I had to smile at myself then, standing there in the sunshine at Forest Hills, with the people strolling casually along the walks, and the great wash of sound rising now from the stadium, now from the grandstand, and sometimes the rasp of an elevated train tearing by, or the rumble of a La Guardia jet in the breezy blue sky. One summer of hard work, and I was already comparing myself with the likes of Virginia Wade.

But I'd learned one thing about myself that summer. I wasn't going to be content with winning a few club tournaments, like Pat, and eventually settling down to a little weekend tennis, like my parents and their friends. If I played at all, it was going to be for real.

There was a roar from the stadium, and I glanced over at the outside scoreboard. Apparently Tanner was in the process of upsetting Stan Smith. With a last reluctant glance at the practice courts, I made my way back up to our seats, where I found my mother and Pat in the midst of a low-pitched but vigorous argument.

"Because I don't want to, that's why!" Pat was saying, as they both squeezed over to let me sit down. "I've got a hard schedule at school this year—"

"You won't be having all that much homework this soon," Mom insisted. "And I did sign you up for it."

"Well, you shouldn't have!"

I knew what they were talking about—the end-of-season tournament at our club, scheduled for the weekend after next. They had this same argument every year, and every year Pat wound up playing in it, and usually winning.

Pat waited until the next point had been played, and then said in a vehement whisper, "It's not as if there's ever any competition, except for Mrs. Whittaker, and she's done something to her knee. I mean, an invitational tournament is one thing, but when it's members-only—"

"So what's wrong with just winning it?" my mother demanded.

"Oh, Mom! Look, why not let Dulcie enter it instead? She's been playing a lot of tennis lately with that Mrs. Travis—"

"Trask," I corrected; but no one heard me.

"You mean you're going to *default*?" My mother sounded as if lightning might strike at any moment.

"Oh, for heaven's sake!" Pat's voice rose. "Look, just stop *leaning* on me, will you?"

People around us were hissing for silence. They both subsided, looking cross.

I stared down at the players, noting dully that although Tanner was playing well, Stan Smith was definitely off his game. Well, I thought, I certainly can't complain about being leaned on—at least not where tennis is concerned.

"The sooner you let other people know you mean business, Dulcie," Mrs. Trask had told me, "the easier things will be for you."

I could see that now, all right. But how to let them know? And what about the rest of my life? That was what I still couldn't figure out.

Later on, when Dad asked me to take Eric down to the bathroom just as the Connors match was beginning, I didn't even protest.

two

THAT SUMMER had started for me like a lot of others before it, with the one big difference that Pat had just gotten her driver's license, and so we were able to spend even more time than usual at the club. With both our parents working, we'd always been dependent on rides from other people during the week. Now it seemed to me that the three of us—Pat, Eric, and I—were practically opening and closing the place on every sunny day. Usually we'd stay until late afternoon, when it was time to go home and start supper and do laundry and cleaning and all the other chores we—but mostly I—were supposed to take care of in Mom's absence.

Pat played tennis, of course. Eric splashed in the

pool with his buddies and charged hot dogs and sodas at the refreshment stand whenever I wasn't looking—which I was supposed to be, Eric being my job for the summer. But I was also supposed to be working on my swimming, lap after boring lap in that boring blue, chlorine-smelling water. Swimming was my sport, according to my parents. Never mind that I'm not built for it (Pat should be the swimmer), and that the club coach had me concentrating on long-distance events these days because even he could see that about all I had going for me was endurance—still, swimming was what Dulcie did. I'd been made to compete in the club meets ever since I was a little kid and more recently in meets with other clubs, and I hated every clammy, wet minute of it.

In fact, I'd begun to hate the club itself, the whole Technicolor scene of bratty kids and glamor-boy lifeguards and lounging women with their cigarettes and gossip and fancy straw hats brought back from Jamaica or St. Croix or wherever. Overfed, over-tanned, underworked. Maybe that isn't fair; it's not a really fancy or fashionable club, not like some of the others around with their golf courses and white-columned clubhouses and name bands on Saturday nights. Our club offers swimming and tennis and an occasional clambake around the pool, and a lot of the members are pretty nice.

What bothers me is, we can't really afford it. That's not something I just found out, it's a point my mother has been making in one way or another for years. Whenever she comes home tired from work (she's a dental nurse) or gets irritated with us kids about something, she'll say, "Listen, why do you think I stand on my feet all day, probably getting varicose veins"—untrue, she has beautiful smooth legs, in fact she has a neat figure for someone her age—"and taking all that guff from that impossible man"—true enough, Dr. Hebert can be a real stinker at times— "except to put a little fun in our lives? Your father earns our daily bread, sure, and I'm not knocking that. But there wouldn't be any jam on it if it wasn't for me, and don't you forget it!"

By which she means things like Pat's piano and tennis lessons and our new clothes, spring and fall, and the family room we added onto the house last year, and excursions like the one to Forest Hills. But above all she means our membership in the club.

Well, maybe I don't care enough about jam, at least not just for its own sake. I know how much my parents enjoy their weekend tennis, and once when the club courts were full, I suggested they try the public courts at the town recreation center. There are six of them, and until recently they were never crowded. My mother just looked down her nose at me and said, "Asphalt? And all those people who don't know one end of a tennis racket from the other? No, *thank* you."

Of course there's Pat's TENNIS—that's the way

I used to think of it, in capital letters—and her friends at the club, and the pro who gives her lessons. But mainly, I guess, the club is a status thing with Mom. I don't think my father cares about that side of it—he has some men's-doubles friends he likes to bum around with, and he gets a kick out of fooling around with Eric in the pool, and that's about it.

Anyway, as usual, our mother worked, and we kids enjoyed the affluent life at the club among a lot of other kids who really could afford it. It's always made me feel a little uncomfortable, and that summer, as I say, I found myself almost hating the place.

Fourth of July weekend came and went, a real heat wave that year, during which Pat got to the semifinals of a tournament in Greenwich and lost. I thought her legs were going to buckle in the final set, and she almost had to be helped off the court. The heat bothers her a lot more than it does me, no matter how many salt pills she swallows before a match. The next week we were back at the club, and the summer began to look endless to me. Eric had a sore throat and wasn't allowed in the pool, so I tried to persuade him to stay home for a change, promising to play games with him, even Monopoly—but no way, the club was where he wanted to be.

"At least you won't have to be watching me all the time," he pointed out. "You can play tennis with Pat."

"Pat's too good for me," I said.

"Well, you hardly ever play any more," said Eric.

And whose fault is that? I thought; but of course it wasn't Eric's, not really. At the last minute I grabbed my sneakers and racket and tossed them into the VW, and we churned off to the club. The weather was hot and sunny, not muggy the way it had been over the Fourth, and after I'd done my laps in the pool, I flopped down on a towel and sunbathed lazily, listening to scraps of conversation around me and not thinking about anything in particular. I was almost asleep when a shadow fell over me, and I blinked up into the face of Pat's friend Laura.

"Hey, Dulcie. The Morrisons are looking for a fourth for mixed doubles. Pat said you might want to play."

"Oh." I sat up, yawning. "Well, I don't know. I don't have any whites with me. . . ."

"That doesn't matter on weekdays," Laura said. "The rule's just for weekends, and they don't even enforce it then. Come on, Dulcie, I said I'd let them know."

I looked at Laura in her immaculate white tennis dress—whatever the rule says, most people, and certainly all the older ones, still turn up in whites—and thought of my red halter top and old denim shorts. But nuts to all that stuff, I thought suddenly, and said, "Okay. Just tell them to wait while I change."

The Morrisons were a youngish married couple

who played pretty good tennis, and who'd always been quite nice to me—talking *to* me, not just through me, if you know what I mean—and whose kids were less bratty than most. But I didn't know who my partner would be, and I felt a little nervous as I walked over to the courts. I saw Pat and Laura getting ready to play doubles with two other older girls and wished for the tenth time that summer that more of my own friends belonged to the club. But except for my best friend Amy, who was away at camp, none of them did, and because of the guest fees —which had risen this year—I didn't get to invite anyone very often.

The Morrisons—in white, naturally—were warming up with a funny-looking paunchy man in a checked shirt and floppy Bermuda shorts who announced cheerfully that he was in lousy shape. "I'll take care of the strategy, Dulcie," he told me. "You just take care of the shots."

"Don't listen to him, Dulcie," Mr. Morrison called. "Sam's an old pro. Between the two of you, you'll probably run us off the court."

"Old being the operative word," Sam grunted, sending up a lob for Mr. Morrison to smash. I smiled politely at him over my shoulder as I turned for a backhand Mrs. Morrison had hit to me, and thought, Oh, for Pete's sake, why did I ever get into this, I'd be better off working out against the backboard by myself; or even swimming.

"A lefty, hey?" said Sam (I never did learn his

last name). "Well, good, you take the ad court. That way I won't have to scramble for backhands."

I was surprised; I hadn't played much mixed doubles, but usually it was the man who automatically took the left-hand court, as being the stronger player, more likely to return service well in a deuce game. Still, in this case maybe *I* was the stronger player—and certainly it made sense to have both our forehands on the outside. When we'd finished rallying and the Morrisons had won the spin of the racket, I moved obediently over to the left.

"Up, Dulcie," Sam said, motioning me forward into the service court. "We'll mow 'em down at the net. That's point one of our game plan."

I felt doubtful, but did as he directed. In fact, I loved playing net whenever I was practicing with someone, but in an actual game I hardly ever seemed to get the chance. Mostly I'd played singles—with Pat when we were younger, before she got so serious about her tennis, more recently with Amy and other kids my age—and I hadn't yet learned to follow my serve in to the net. As for doubles . . . well, I hadn't actually played much tennis of any kind this summer. I reminded myself, and took a firm grip on my racket as Mr. Morrison fired in his first serve.

It was a good hard serve, to Sam's backhand. He didn't even try to block it back, but instead lifted a weak-looking lob over Mrs. Morrison's head, too high for her to reach, but not high enough to give

Mr. Morrison much time to get to it—and in fact he didn't. The ball bounced two feet inside the baseline for a winner. A peculiar winner, maybe, but a winner.

"Finest shot in mixed doubles," Sam said with satisfaction. "The blooper."

"Darn you, Sam!" said Mrs. Morrison. "You know I can't go after those."

"Exactly," he said, grinning at her.

Mr. Morrison served more gently to me (which is something I don't like about mixed doubles—I'd much rather hit a hard ball than a soft one) and I got off a good return deep into his backhand corner which he mis-hit into the net. "Ouch!" he said.

"Just lucky," I said, which wasn't true; if the serve's to my forehand and I can get some topspin on it, that's a shot I can almost always make. Mrs. Trask really blasted me later for that kind of talk. "There's no such thing as luck in this game, Dulcie," she said. "Or to put it another way, you make your own luck."

Love–30, and Mr. Morrison missed his first serve to Sam. The second had a slice on it but not much power, and Sam hit a cross-court return that just skimmed the net. It wasn't a hard shot, though it had a good angle, and I started to move back defensively, away from the drive I knew was coming from Mr. Morrison's strong forehand.

"No, stay up!" yelled Sam, who had followed his return to the net. With both of us covering the net, Mr. Morrison tried a shot down my alley—probably forgetting that was my forehand side. I reached for it and smacked it across the center of the court. Mrs. Morrison had moved back, though, and she lifted a good lob over our heads.

"Yours," said Sam, unnecessarily; I was already tearing after the ball. It bounced high, just short of the baseline, and I had a shot I really like to make—a backhand drive on a high bouncer that I let drop and then hit as hard and flat as I can, usually surprising an opponent who expects a return lob, or at least a fairly soft shot hit under the ball. But this time, maybe because I was still a little nervous, I hit it resoundingly into the net.

"Wow!" said my partner.

"I'm sorry," I said. "I guess that was a dumb thing to do."

"Not at all. It's just that few people can do it at all. It takes a strong wrist and forearm. *And* nerve." He grinned at me, but I could feel him looking at me thoughtfully as I took up my position to receive serve.

Maybe figuring my first return had been a fluke, Mr. Morrison served again to my forehand, and again I drove the ball into his backhand corner. This time he got his racket on it solidly, but hit the ball within Sam's reach at the net. He slapped it down behind Mrs. Morrison for the put-away.

"Five-forty," Sam crowed. "We've got 'em now, Dulcie."

In answer to which, Mr. Morrison aced him.

My turn to receive—a harder serve than before, and to my backhand. I meant to hit it cross-court, but didn't get my shoulder around far enough, and instead drove the ball straight at Mrs. Morrison at the net. Taken by surprise, she stepped back, holding her racket protectively across her body, and the ball banged off it and into the net. "Oh, really, Jean!" she said to herself in disgust.

"Nice going," Sam said to me as we changed courts.

"Well, that last shot . . ." I shook my head.

"Yeah, well, maybe you didn't mean to do it, but sometimes that's a smart play, you know—just hit the ball as hard as you can, straight at the net player. The old belt-buckle shot. You'd be surprised how many points you can win that way."

Sam's serve was as unorthodox as everything else about him—not beautiful, certainly, but surprisingly effective. He put a devilish spin on the ball and seemed to be able to place it wherever he wanted to.

In fact, as the set went on, I began to realize what a really elegant doubles player he was, despite the apparent clumsiness of his strokes and the fact that he never seemed to move very far or fast. He was always in position; he never wasted energy slamming the ball when a short deft shot would do. Indeed, most of his put-aways were lightly hit— angled shots that caught a player going the wrong way or bounced just behind his heels or simply dropped dead over the net. Once, when I had an easy overhead and smashed the ball out, trying for the baseline corner, he pointed out mildly that with the whole court open, a shorter shot would have done just as well; and of course he was right.

We took the first set 6–3, and would have won it by more except for my miserable serve. I served the ball into the net, I served it three feet over the service line, or into the alley, or sometimes into the wrong court entirely. Altogether, in two service games, I double-faulted five times. After the last of these, Sam saw me biting my lip—maybe he even saw the tears of frustration in my eyes—and said, "Okay, Dulcie, so you need to work on your serve. For now, don't try to be so fancy. Just throw the ball up, hit it, and put it in play."

I tried, and did a little better, though it was a silly kid's kind of serve, just poking the ball over the net that way; and I was embarrassed when the Morrisons either hit it out or into the net the first few times—something that's all too easy to do with a soft pat-ball serve. But then they got the range (if that's the word) and began short-courting me with their returns, so that I really had to scramble to get to the ball at all. They were both playing well in that second set, especially Mrs. Morrison, and she and I had some long baseline rallies that were fun. I felt myself relaxing, getting into the rhythm of my ground strokes; and the net play was pure pleasure, the satis-

fying solid *thwack* of strings against the ball, the crouching and spinning that's almost like a dance when your game is going well. I realized I'd almost forgotten how much I loved playing tennis.

We were at 2–all in the third set, having finally won the second 7–5, when Mrs. Morrison looked at her watch and said she'd have to stop. "I've got to go rescue the kids from the play group—or do I mean rescue the counselor. Anyway, it's time for their lunch. And anyway, I'm pooped. Whew, that sun is terrific!"

I came out of my trance and saw how hot the others looked, their clothes stuck to them with sweat. Sam's face was a fiery red under his spiky graying hair.

"Okay," he agreed. "This old man has had it, much as I hate to admit it, and you two don't look much better. My partner here is the only one who doesn't even seem winded. I bet you could go on playing all day, couldn't you, Dulcie?"

They all smiled at me, and I felt suddenly shy again. "It was fun," I said. "Thanks for letting me play."

"Listen, you made the game," Mr. Morrison said as we walked over to the sidelines. "I had no idea you were such a tennis player, Dulcie."

"Neither did I," said his wife. "I mean, I've watched your sister Pat play many times, but I've hardly ever seen you on the courts."

"Oh, well," I said. "I just don't get around to tennis too often, I guess."

"Well, you ought to," Mr. Morrison said, toweling off his face. "Are you taking lessons?"

"Not now. I did when I was a kid. I mean . . ." I stopped, feeling foolish.

"Listen, on the tennis court you're no kid," Sam said, "you're a tiger. I don't know what your sister's tennis is like, but you've got a real instinct for the game, Dulcie. You ought to work on it."

"Yes, you really should," the Morrisons agreed.

They were all looking at me, and I didn't know what to say. I felt flushed and hot, much hotter than I'd felt on the court. "My sister Pat . . ." I began.

"Never *mind* your sister," Sam said, cuffing me lightly. "So she's a genius, maybe you're a genius too. And I bet she isn't as pretty as you."

I saw the Morrisons exchange glances, and there was an awkward little silence. Then Mrs. Morrison hitched her tennis sweater over her shoulders, handed her racket to her husband, and said, "Well, I'm off to get the kids. See you back at the house, boys."

The men went off toward the parking lot, and Mrs. Morrison and I walked back over to the pool area, where there's a section set aside around a little wading pool for the five-and-under kids, under the supervision of a college girl. I realized I'd forgotten all about Eric and glanced around for him guiltily, but he was just standing talking to one of the life guards over by the pool house. And eating a hot dog, what else?

Mrs. Morrison sighed, looking at the knot of little kids by the wading pool, and said, "I wish I felt happier about this play group deal. It seems to me all they do is throw water at each other and eat graham crackers and play Simon Says. I'd hoped Molly would begin learning to swim this summer— she's five-and-a-half, and she's crazy about the water. But that's not part of the program, it seems. You're a swimmer, Dulcie—do you think that's too young to start?"

"No. I'd say that's a good age, if she really wants to learn."

"What I should have done," Mrs. Morrison said, more to herself than me, "was hire a good sitter this summer, who could have taken them over to the recreation center—it's practically next door to us— and really *done* things with them. There's a perfectly good pool there, and a playground. . . . Oh, well, I suppose it's too late to find anyone now."

Then she looked at me. *"Dulcie!* How about you? Oh, you'd be just perfect! I know you're young —forgive me, sweetie, but you are only thirteen, aren't you?—but you're a responsible type and good with kids and. . . . It's not as if they're infants any more, Kim's almost three, so you wouldn't have to cope with diapers and bottles and all that nonsense. Seriously, Dulcie, could you do it? I'd pay you the going rate, and it'd only be mornings—except it would be great if you could stay long enough to give them their lunch. Or do you already have a job?"

I looked at Mrs. Morrison's open enthusiastic face—she isn't exactly pretty, but energy practically crackles out of her eyes and smile—and said regretfully, "Well, sort of. My brother Eric. I mean, I'm supposed to look after him. . . . I'd really love to baby-sit for you, Mrs. Morrison, but I don't see how I can. Eric would have to come along with me, and . . ." I shrugged, to show how impossible that would be.

"What about Pat? Can't she look after Eric?"

"Oh, she has her tennis, and . . . well, I don't think she'd . . . well, that just wouldn't work out." How do you explain your family to someone else? As I said before, Pat had her territory, and I had mine, that had been established long ago. I said lamely, "I mean, she couldn't exactly be playing tennis and watching Eric at the pool at the same time."

But Mrs. Morrison persisted. "Why does someone have to watch Eric at the pool? That's the lifeguards' job, after all. He's over six, isn't he?"

"Seven." The pool rules specify that kids under six have to be accompanied by their parents or a sitter.

"And he swims pretty well, doesn't he?"

"He can when he wants to," I admitted. "Mostly he just fools around."

"Well, then!" said Mrs. Morrison. "No problem. You come work for me in the mornings and earn some money; meanwhile, Eric swims and Pat plays tennis. And then, if you like, I'll run you over here afterwards. Who knows, you might even get in some tennis of your own." She smiled, but she was watching me closely. "That is, if you'd really like the job, Dulcie."

Her little girls had spotted her and came running over, Molly leaping ahead with her straight blonde hair flying, and Kim struggling to keep up on her baby-fat legs. Molly flung her arms around her mother's waist, saying couldn't they go home now, and Kim fell down and began to cry. Automatically I reached for her, set her on her feet, and stood stroking her soft light hair, avoiding Mrs. Morrison's questioning glance.

At last I said, "I really would like to do it, Mrs. Morrison. In fact I'd love it. I—I'll talk to my parents about it and let you know, okay?"

"Okay." She gave my hand a quick firm shake, as if everything were all settled. "And now I'd better get these two characters home. Molly!" Molly was already streaking off toward the parking lot. "Molly, come back here! Where's your towel and your sandals? And what about Kim's things? Molly!"

"Thanks again for the tennis, Mrs. Morrison," I said; but I don't think she heard me.

three

"BUT DULCIE," my mother said, as I'd known she would, "what about Eric?"

"Eric doesn't really need me, Mom. He has his own friends at the club, and the lifeguards are good this year—they're really strict with the younger kids. About the only thing *I* do is try and stop him from eating all the time."

"Oh . . ." She dismissed this with a wave of her hand, even though she's the one who throws a fit when the club bills come in. "I still say he's too young to be left on his own. And what about your swimming?"

I started to say I could get in my laps in the afternoons; but something—the good tennis that day,

Mrs. Morrison's assumption that I was old enough to make some choices on my own—made me blurt out: "Mom, I've *had* it with swimming! I'm not that good at it anyway, so what's the point in going on with it? You just ask Mr. Garcia"—he was the coach—"and he'll tell you the same."

There was a shocked silence, as though I'd said I no longer liked sunshine or Christmas or something. We were in the air-conditioned family room after supper, my mother resting with her feet up on the couch, my father in his reclining chair watching TV. Eric was outside playing, and you could hear Pat practicing her scales on the piano in the living room.

"Now listen, Dulcie—" my mother began; but Dad got up and turned down the volume of the TV, saying over his shoulder, "How long have you felt this way, Boots?" Boots is his old pet name for me, because when I was little I hated wearing shoes of any kind and especially my rain boots. I still do, for that matter, and go barefoot whenever I'm out of my parents' sight.

"A long time," I muttered. "The last couple of years, anyway."

"Well, why didn't you ever say anything?"

"I don't know. . . . I knew you wanted me to do it, and—well, there isn't that much else to do at the club anyway." I looked up at him and said in a rush, "If you'd only let me go in for diving, I would have liked that—but swimming's so boring."

It was the wrong thing to say. Diving was an old issue between us. I thought I would have been a good diver, but my parents thought it was too dangerous a sport for a girl.

My father frowned. He said, "Well, anyway, I agree with your mother about this job with the Morrisons. If it's the money you care about—well, maybe we can increase your allowance a little. I know you do a lot of work around here, Dulcie, and I suppose inflation is hard on you kids, too."

He shook his head and began telling my mother some story about a high-priced line of garden chairs he carries at the hardware store, and my mother interrupted to tell him about the price of canned goods at the supermarket, and I thumped myself down on the new orange vinyl hassock Mom had bought last week and said loudly: "You're always talking about our learning to be independent and making our own way in life. Well, this is my chance to start, even if it is just a baby-sitting job!"

They both stared at me. My mother said, "Dulcie, this isn't like you at all! What on earth's gotten into you?"

I was surprised at myself too, but I went charging on. "Or maybe you just mean Pat, not me. I'm the one who's supposed to learn to cook and keep house and have dates, until it's time to get married and do *more* cooking and *more* housekeeping while some *man* takes care of me, and all because I'm—pretty, or something!" And I burst into tears.

"Well, of all the crazy things to cry about," said my mother with a snort.

"Sounds like a bit of women's lib in the air," my father said, and chucked me gently under the chin. "Now come on, Dulcie—of course we want you to have lots of opportunities in your life. But you can't go against your own nature, you know. It's not just that you're pretty, Boots—you're sweet and generous too, and you like doing things for other people. Now don't you? And you *like* cooking and cleaning and keeping a house tidy, all those things. Don't you?"

I nodded blindly.

"Now, nobody's more in favor of independence for women than I am," he went on with an indulgent smile. "But what does that really mean? It means doing your own thing, as you kids say. And going out and having a career, competing with men, maybe giving up a home and family for the sake of something you care about more—well, that takes a lot of drive and ambition, Dulcie, and people are different, not everybody's made that way. Do you understand what I mean?"

I nodded again. But I do have it! I wanted to say—the drive and the ambition and the caring; only I don't know yet what it's *for*.

"Yes," my mother put in, in what for her was an

unusually mild tone. "I'm not the domestic type my- self, as you know. Oh, maybe I gripe a lot about my job and being away from the house all day, but the truth is I'd rather work in a bobby pin factory than stay home baking and waxing floors. But I have great respect for the women who do stay home and do those things well, Dulcie. In fact it makes me furious to hear people putting down the average, ordinary housewife, the way they're always doing these days. Why, I think being a housewife is one of the most truly *creative* things you can do!"

I almost smiled at that. The truth is, my mother is just plain lazy when it comes to housework and is honestly a little in awe of anyone who actually en- joys putting some effort into it.

Pat came into the room then, raised her eye- brows at the emotional atmosphere and went over to the bookshelves, dropping a hand on the top of my head in passing. "Hi, Cinderella," she said, an old joke between us that always annoys our parents.

My father cleared his throat. "We were just talking about this job of Dulcie's," he said, and I felt a spark of hope at the way he put it.

"Job?"

Pat turned to look at us. The late sunlight slant- ing through the big windows of the room cruelly illuminated the right side of her face, with the long scar that curves down from her temple almost to the corner of her mouth. The scar isn't really ugly in itself, it's just a line; but it does have the effect of making her face look sort of lopsided, except when she smiles.

Dad explained about Mrs. Morrison's offer, adding, "But of course, aside from anything else, it's too much responsibility for a thirteen-year-old."

Which at least was a new argument.

Pat said calmly, "That's ridiculous, Dad. Look at all the responsibility Dulcie's used to having around here. I think she'd be great at the job, and she ought to take it. As for Eric, I can check on him from time to time, but it'll do him good to be on his own for a change."

Mom and Dad were looking sort of stunned. Pat went on: "And as far as the afternoons are concerned, if Dulcie wants to come over to the club, fine. If she'd rather stay home and have some time to herself, after taking care of a couple of little kids all morning, no sweat. I can still keep an eye on Eric."

"Well, Pat, that's very generous of you—" my father began, after a moment's silence, but Mom interrupted:

"What if it rains?"

I said quickly, "Oh, if it rains, Mrs. Morrison probably won't need me."

Pat said, "I can't play tennis when it's raining, anyway. I'll find something to do with Eric. Now that I've got my license, I can take him to the movies, stuff like that."

"Well. . . ." Dad ran a hand through his dark hair that's still thick and glossy, like Pat's. "I must say, a job's a job in my book and never mind the weather. If Mrs. Morrison's going to hire you, Dulcie, it should be for every day, rain or shine. You've got to be businesslike about these things," he added sternly; and I knew I'd won. Or rather Pat and I had won. "I also think she should pay you a little more than the going rate, since you're committing that much time to her. Just remember, Boots, there'll be days when you won't feel like going, when you'll be tired or have had it with the kids; but you'll have to show up just the same."

"I know, Daddy," I said meekly.

Eric, who'd come into the room during the discussion about rain, said, "I wouldn't mind staying home *all* the time if I had a dog."

"Oh, no," my mother said, swinging her legs off the couch and sitting up with a groan. "Do we have to go through this again?"

But Eric held his ground—literally, his whole body looking stubborn and braced for argument, his grimy fists planted on his hips, legs apart in their old jeans and basketball sneakers. "Dad said maybe when I got old enough. Well, I'm old enough *now*. I could take care of him all by myself."

Dad said, "There's an awful lot of work involved, old man. Maybe in another year or two—"

"Messes," said my mother. "Dog hairs. Yapping.

43

Vet bills, and Lord knows we can do without *those*."

"It wouldn't have to be a big dog," Eric pleaded, as if this had anything to do with anything. "It wouldn't get in the way."

"Oh, they're the worst," Mom told him wearily. "It's the little ones that yap the loudest. And bite your ankles, and get up on the furniture. No, Eric, for the last time, absolutely not."

Eric's eyes filled with tears, but he didn't cry. I'll give him that; he may do a lot of begging and wheedling, but he hardly ever cries. "But Daddy *said*—"

"Not this year," my father said firmly.

I could see both of them trying not to look at him. They really hate denying Eric anything, and Pat says if it weren't for the fact that Mom dislikes dogs—as well as cats and guinea pigs and hamsters, all the pets we'd yearned for over the years—they'd probably have presented him with a puppy on a velvet cushion long since.

I heard myself say: "I could help take care of it. I mean, if you did get Eric a dog."

"Oh, *Dulcie!*" said my mother, and Pat said, "Dulcie, you must be out of your mind!"

My father said, "When?"

"Well . . ."

"You're a working girl now, remember."

"But that's just mornings. I could still—"

"No." He went over to the TV and turned the volume back up.

44

"But Dad . . ." I wanted to say how much good it would do Eric to have something to care about besides himself, and be responsible for.

"I said no, Dulcie. And what about in the fall, when you're in school all day? What happens to the dog then? Besides, if you took care of it, it would wind up being more your dog than Eric's, anyway."

Well, all that was probably true enough. Another year, as Dad said. But on my way out of the room, I put my arm around Eric's shoulders and whispered, "Maybe we can get another turtle at least, Eric. Or two, so they can keep each other company."

"The last one died," Eric said mournfully.

"Well, but if we had two . . . who knows, the other one might have died just because it got bored. Bored to *death*," I said, and got a reluctant grin from Eric. I smacked him lightly on the seat of his jeans and said, "Go on, now, brush your teeth and get ready for bed, and I'll read to you for a while if you want."

Later, as Pat and I were getting ready for bed ourselves, she said, "Why on earth did you stick up for Eric over the dog business, Dulcie? You know how they spoil him anyway and always wind up giving in to him."

"Over the wrong things, though. I mean, babying him is wrong, but . . ." I pulled my nightgown over my head, trying to find words to explain what I meant.

Pat snorted, sounding exactly like our mother.

"You're just pure *mush* inside, Dulcie, you know that? . . . I wonder why they do," she went on, before I could protest. "Baby him, I mean."

"Well, he's the youngest . . ."

"*And* the boy."

As if that settled it, she flopped down on her bed and stared out the open window into the summer darkness sprinkled with the lights of neighboring houses. The room felt stifling after the chill of the air-conditioned family room, and the heat made it seem even more crowded than usual with all our gear. We try to keep things neat, but it's not a very big room, and what with Pat's books and records and paints, and my posters and stuffed animals and the old doll house I won't part with, even though Pat says it's a sexist toy, it always looks sort of jumbled and confused.

Dad suggested putting up a partition last year, to give us each some privacy, but we said no, neither of us would be able to breathe in the space we'd have left. We never talked about it, but I think Pat and I both felt at least some of the money that went into the family room should have been spent on another bedroom instead. The family room's very nice, and Mom's had a lot of fun fixing it up; but we could have done over the basement much more cheaply and still had something left over. I even suggested that to Mom once, but I guess it was the same as the country-club membership—she wanted something that would *show*.

I got into bed with just a sheet over me and turned out my light. "What did you mean, about Eric being the boy?"

"Oh, Dulcie!" Pat turned over onto her back. "Can't you see how much that matters to them? Why else did they have another baby six years after you were born, with both of them working? Because they had two daughters and they wanted a *son,* that's why."

"Well, what's wrong with that?" But I thought about it and said slowly, "If you mean they . . . discriminate, or whatever the word is—well, they let you go your own way, don't they?" I wondered if Pat had overheard any of the earlier part of our conversation in the family room. "I mean, they want you to be independent and have your own interests and—"

"Yes," Pat said. "And you know why."

She spoke calmly; her bitterness wasn't directed at me. And of course I did know why. In spite of what I'd said to my parents, I guess I'd realized long ago that the main reason they were always encouraging Pat and praising her achievements was their fear that she could never have a so-called normal life as a woman, because of her face. But it had never occurred to me that Pat might resent them for it, much less that she might actually want that kind of life for herself.

A car went by outside, trailing a faint beat of rock music from its radio. I wondered now how Pat really felt about never going to dances or out on dates—whether she was as resigned as she seemed. Maybe that's the trouble, I thought; she's too resigned. I know if I were a boy, I'd be scared to ask Pat for a date; she can seem so cold and aloof sometimes, as if she didn't need or want anybody's company but her own.

"Oh, well." Pat got up to brush her hair in front of the mirror. "Anyway, as far as Eric's concerned, he's going to have to start growing up fast with me in charge. I'm just not as patient as you are."

"I know," I said seriously. "And it'll be good for him. . . . Listen, Pat"—I raised myself on one elbow—"thanks a lot for what you said tonight. About my job, I mean. But honestly, if Eric does give you any trouble over at the club, interfering with your tennis or anything, I'll tell Mrs. Morrison to find somebody else. I mean, it's not that big a deal, just a baby-sitting job, and your tennis—"

"Tennis!" Pat slammed down her brush and turned around to glare at me. "Sometimes I get so sick and tired of all this everlasting fuss about tennis! Do you know *I* tried to get a job this summer? Mother's helper, waitress—I didn't care. But of course nobody would hire me. I'd scare the customers away, or give the kiddies nightmares."

"Oh, Pat!"

My eyes filled with tears; I wanted to jump up and put my arms around her, to try to comfort her somehow. But I knew when she got in this kind of mood—which fortunately wasn't very often—she didn't want anyone to touch her, or even sympathize with her. Especially me, maybe. But I pushed that thought away. Over the years I'd learned not to think certain thoughts about me and Pat.

Instead I swallowed hard and said, "But—is that really the way you feel about tennis? I mean, I thought you liked it."

"I do, I enjoy the game itself. And I've gotten so I don't even mind the tournaments, and all those people looking at me. . . . But it's Mom's and Dad's whole attitude. I mean, you don't see them trying to push me into any real competition, do you? No, they're happy to have me around as a kind of—minor celebrity, with some trophies they can stick on the mantel."

"But . . ."

"Oh, I know I'm not all that good anyway," Pat said. "But that's not the point. The point is, I could be another Maureen Connolly or Chris Evert, and they'd still want to keep things, oh, ladylike and in proportion. Amateur. You know how Dad feels about the women pros—he likes watching them play, but as far as he's concerned they're a bunch of money-grubbing, unfeminine freaks."

She took up the brush again and began attacking her hair. I said curiously, "Would you want to be a pro, if you could?"

"Not particularly. There are too many other

things I'm interested in, and it's a rough life, from what you hear. Aside from talent, you have to be a lot more competitive than I am. More aggressive. I mean, I like to do things well, and if I win, fine, but I just don't care all that much about beating out other people. . . . Hey, I forgot to ask you, how was your game with the Morrisons today? Your partner looked like a real weirdo."

"Oh, it was fun," I said, rather absently. I was thinking what a good-looking girl Pat was from the back, standing there in her shortie pajamas with her shining, thick hair falling over her shoulders and her long brown legs, like Mom's. "He was quite good, actually."

"I looked over once or twice, and you seemed to be tearing all over the place and really whamming the ball." Pat got into bed and said as she turned out her light, "You really ought to play more, Dulcie. I bet you'd be good."

I smiled wryly to myself in the darkness. People seemed to have been saying that to me all day. But at least, I thought, turning over and trying to find a cool spot on the pillow, nobody's telling me to take up swimming.

four

MY JOB with the Morrisons turned out to be a good
deal more work than I'd expected; but I didn't mention this to my parents, who would have insisted on
my asking for a raise—and actually most of the extra
work was of my own making. It was mainly that Mrs.
Morrison had sort of a casual attitude about housework. She'd go dashing off to meetings and tennis
dates and volunteer work at the hospital with the
breakfast dishes still in the sink or the beds unmade
or the kids' laundry waiting to be folded and put
away—if she'd even got around to doing it in the
first place.

"Oh, please don't bother about the mess," she'd
say as she took off. "I'll get to it later." But when she

came back, it was "Oh, Dulcie, you're a lamb, thanks so much," as if she wasn't really surprised; or maybe just not very interested.

Even when she spent the morning at home, she always seemed to be busy on the phone or outside working in the garden. She was quite active in community affairs, the kind of thing my mother never had time for, even if she'd had the interest; though when Mrs. Morrison talked to me about the new kindergarten curriculum or a paper-recycling project or plans for the new clinic at the hospital, she made it all sound kind of suspenseful and exciting—not at all the way my mother thought of "do-gooding."

As for the garden, there were flowers everywhere, and a big fenced-in vegetable garden, and a tiny, geometrical plot of herbs by the kitchen door. The house was always filled with bowls and vases of flowers, even when the tables they sat on needed dusting. I couldn't help comparing all this extravagant color and fragrance with our own few lilac and hydrangea bushes, and the token bed of marigolds and petunias my mother plants each spring and I always wind up weeding.

But of course this was country-club territory, big solid houses on two acres or more, with circular driveways and flagstone terraces and sports cars in the garages. Our house is just an ordinary frame house near the center of town, in a neighborhood where people have yards instead of lawns, with maybe a grill and some plastic chairs out back, and mostly drive Fords and Chevys.

Anyhow, by the end of a week or so, I had things pretty much down to a routine. Mrs. Morrison would pick me up at nine every morning, and I'd spend an hour cleaning up the kitchen and doing whatever else seemed most urgent before I took the kids over to the recreation center. Even if Mrs. Morrison didn't care, it gave me an uneasy feeling to go off leaving things in a mess—like starting the day without brushing my teeth or combing my hair. Compulsive, Pat calls me, and I guess I am, about some things.

Around ten, I'd get Molly and Kim organized—bathing suits and towels and their terrycloth robes, a snack for later on, Kim's blue pail, some extra toys for her to play with if she got bored—and we'd set off for the center. As Mrs. Morrison had said, it was practically next door, an old estate the town had bought some years before and converted for public use. We walked a little way down the road, cut across a field, and there we were at the big wrought-iron gates. Except for a carriage house used for staff offices, all the original buildings had been torn down; but the huge old trees survived, shading the playground area where we usually spent the first hour.

It was a big playground with the traditional assortment of swings and slides and jungle gyms, and also some new modular play equipment in bright-colored plastic—oddly shaped domes and tunnels and pyramids for crawling over or under or through. These intrigued me, but most of the kids seemed to prefer the old-fashioned apparatus. Maybe modern designers forget how much children love just plain old speed and motion.

Anyway, at around eleven, we'd gather up our things and go on over to the big bath house to change for swimming. At first the little girls were bewildered and shy about the whole routine, the dogtags and lockers and the big boys who ran yelling through the wet cement corridors, flicking towels at each other; but pretty soon they got used to it, and when the attendant began remembering their names, they felt almost as much at home as they had in the politer atmosphere of the club.

The pool was Olympic size, and every once in a while, when the kids were safely out of the water to dry off, I'd swim a few laps just for fun. In fact, now that nobody was actually making me swim, I found myself enjoying it—or I would have if the pool hadn't been so crowded; I was always bumping into someone and having to apologize. Quite a few kids I knew from school showed up from time to time, but I kept my promise to Mrs. Morrison and didn't fool around with them or get involved in long conversations. Being a lifeguard, she said, was a full-time job —and in that mob it certainly was. I had to keep my eyes glued simultaneously on Kim at the shallow end —mostly she just staggered around filling her blue pail with water and dumping it out again into the pool gutter—and on Molly plunging around in the excited mass of older kids beyond.

As for the swimming lessons, Molly turned out to be too apt a pupil, if anything. I started her out cautiously with the dead man's float, taught her to float on her back, and then showed her the dog paddle. This may have been a mistake—she was so delighted at being able to move about in the water on her own that I had trouble making her stay still long enough to begin teaching her the crawl and the breathing that went with it. Before I knew it, she was jumping in from the side of the pool, and then diving like a little frog. Only when her lips were actually turning blue could I get her out of the water, and even then she would beg me through chattering teeth to go right back in again.

When the twelve o'clock whistle blew, we'd change back into our clothes and return across the sunny field and along the road that smelled of tar in the summer heat, sometimes stopping to pick wildflowers, which Molly would cram into a jelly glass at home and carry off proudly to her room. I made sandwiches for all of us and poured milk, and we had lunch at a table on the screened porch. Kim would begin looking drowsy by the time she got to her second Oreo cookie, and after I'd cleared the table, I'd take her upstairs for her nap. If there was time—I was supposed to be through at one—I'd get Molly settled in the living room or the den with some coloring books or a puzzle, and maybe read to her for a while. She was supposed to take an hour's rest, but I doubt that Mrs. Morrison really enforced this. I had the feeling Molly was probably up and running again by the time I was out of sight.

Well, that was pretty much the pattern of the job throughout the summer, except when the weather turned cold or rainy. Then I'd have the kids finger painting at the kitchen table or blowing bubbles in the bathroom (Mrs. Morrison didn't seem to care what we did as long as the kids were busy and having fun). Or we'd play games in the playroom and build things out of blocks and put on puppet shows. The playroom was well-stocked, but even so, some of those mornings seemed endless to me. I'd find myself thinking about all the work still to be done at home and have to remind myself that at least I was getting paid for acting out the wolf in Little Red Riding Hood. . . .

For the first few days, Mrs. Morrison drove me over to the club after work; but it was soon clear that Eric and Pat were managing fine without me. Eric had struck up a friendship with one of the lifeguards —a case of hero-worship on his part and good nature on the part of the lifeguard—and hardly bothered to say hello to me. Pat had given firm instructions to the man at the refreshment stand about Eric's food consumption, something I'd never quite had the nerve to do. He was limited to a dollar a day, which provided him with lunch and maybe a soda later on, and he didn't seem to be pining away on this diet.

Anyway, now that I didn't have to go to the club any more, I told Mrs. Morrison I'd just as soon walk home after work. It took me about fifteen minutes, a lot of it uphill, but after the morning with the kids I needed some time to unwind; and anyway I like walking. I couldn't get used to my new freedom at first, or the emptiness and silence of our house when I got there. It took me several days to realize I didn't have to go straight home if I didn't want to—I could go back over to the recreation center for a couple of hours and see the kids there, and still have plenty of time to get my chores done at home.

So I swam in the big pool, and sunbathed, and even tried some diving (from the low board), and talked to Susie Camero and Sharon Wright and some of the boys that hung around—and all the while, in a funny nagging way, I was conscious of the tennis courts that stretched away beyond the pool enclosure. Through the wire mesh of the fence and the stand of evergreens that separated the two areas, I could just make out the quick, darting figures of the players, and sometimes hear the solid thud of a well-hit ball.

One day I took my tennis racket along to the Morrisons', and a can of balls, and after work, instead of heading back to the pool, I went straight over to the courts. I felt kind of strange and furtive about it, hoping the other kids wouldn't see me. For one thing, Sharon had just taken up tennis and might feel hurt that I hadn't asked her to play—and how could I explain to her that I didn't want to waste time playing with a beginner? For another, I was afraid they'd think I was playing here on the public courts to avoid comparison with Pat. They all knew we belonged to a country club and couldn't understand why I wasn't living it up there instead of hanging around here "with us peasants," as Susie put it.

But mainly, I guess, I knew I wanted to work really hard on my tennis if I played at all, and I didn't want them to see me getting that involved with something. It wasn't part of my image, you might say—easygoing Dulcie, always ready to laugh at somebody else's jokes, always going along with other people's plans, never arguing or getting intense or making waves. . . .

My destination that first day was the long backboard that had been built as a separate facility beyond the last of the six courts. There was a strip of asphalt in front of it, about a half-court in depth, and room for five or six players to practice at once, as long as you didn't get too many little kids hitting balls all over the place and tripping you up.

I chose a spot at the far side, dumped my rolled-up towel and shoulder bag on the grass, opened the can of balls, and began hitting forehands steadily and methodically against the splintery green wood—trying to catch the ball on the first bounce each time, working first on a flat stroke, then on topspin, as I'd seen Pat do. It's always a temptation when you're hitting against a backboard to let the ball bounce several times; but that doesn't do anything for your timing or footwork, and you tend to hit the ball much lower than you would in actual play.

After a while I switched to the backhand—same routine, except that I was also trying to work on my backhand lob, which is pretty frustrating to do against a backboard, even a high one. I hit it gently, just trying to get the feel of the stroke, not aiming for height; but even so the balls kept sailing over the top of the backboard, and I'd have to go chase them down in the parking lot beyond.

I gave that up finally and began working on my serve, or rather on the stroke itself, since of course there was no way of telling how the ball would bounce on a court—in, out, or smack into the net. By now, worse luck, there was a small boy practicing next to me, charging around energetically and missing the ball most of the time, sometimes scrambling practically under my feet to retrieve it. He only had one ball, and it was a relief whenever he hit it over the backboard and was gone for a while to look for it.

I gritted my teeth and kept on whacking away at my serve, but it just didn't feel right. I couldn't seem to keep a solid grip on my racket as I made contact with the ball, and I mis-hit it more often than not.

I tried tossing the ball up more to the left, more to the right, more in front of me; I tried a long back-swing, and a short one; I tried keeping both feet on the ground as I hit the ball, I tried stepping into it. Then I decided maybe I was throwing the ball too high in the first place, and went back to working on my toss.

"Oh, *nuts!*" I said at last, as the little boy next to me hit his ball into my territory for the fiftieth time. I caught it and gave it back to him, and he hung his head, mumbling something apologetic. "Hey, I didn't mean you," I said, and smiled at him. He was a cute, tow-headed kid about Eric's age. At the moment he looked sweaty and discouraged and stubborn all at once, and I couldn't help admiring his persistence with that one miserable, grimy tennis ball.

"Let me see how you're holding your racket," I said, and he held it out uncertainly. I showed him the correct forehand grip and how to stand, and after a few false starts he actually hit a clean straight forehand at the backboard, and then another. His whole face lit up with pleasure, but fell again as he swung and missed the ball entirely.

"Never mind," I said. "Your swing was right, and that's the important thing. You just keep working on that, and you'll be surprised how much better you get." I was zipping my racket back into its cover as I spoke, and as an afterthought I handed him one of my tennis balls. "Here—you can keep this to practice with. Yours is really pretty dead."

"Don't you need it?" He looked up at me anxiously.

"No. I've got plenty more at home," I assured him, thinking of Pat's dozens and dozens of practice balls. Of course now that I was earning some money, I could afford to buy balls of my own, a can or two at least—brand new fuzzy yellow tennis balls with the manufacturer's name still clear and unmarred. . . . I turned away, saying, "Maybe next time I see you I can show you how to hit your backhand," and almost collided with a woman standing on the grass near where I'd dropped my towel and shoulder bag.

"I've been watching you," she said in a severe voice, as though she were accusing me of something.

I looked around to see if she meant somebody else; but her eyes behind thick dark glasses seemed to be fixed on my face. I gave a nervous laugh and said, "I'm afraid there wasn't much to watch."

"Oh, yes," the woman said, nodding to herself. "There was a good deal. Your serve, of course, is hopelessly confused. Or to put it another way, you're hopelessly confused about your serve."

"Well, I—"

"But that can be remedied. I don't know who taught you to try a twist serve in the first place, you'll never have the height for it, but . . ." She shrugged, and asked abruptly, "Do you play here often? I'm sure I haven't seen you before."

"No. We belong to a club where I usually play. I was just—"

"Which club?"

I told her, and she shook her head dismissively. "Jack Phillips. No wonder." He was the tennis pro at the club.

I don't know why I didn't get mad at that point —Jack's really a nice guy, and he's helped Pat a lot —or why I didn't just walk away from this peculiar conversation. There's something spooky about finding someone's been watching you without your knowing it; but even aside from that, you'd think I would have resented the cool, impersonal way this strange woman kept firing questions at me.

Yet there was a kind of authority in her manner that held me—that and the fact that she didn't *look* at all spooky or peculiar, except perhaps for the thickness of the glasses that hid her eyes. I'm no good at guessing grown-ups' ages, but I'd say she was about fifty, tall and sort of elegant-looking, without that dry, dieted-out look some older women seem to get. She wore a pale blue linen suit and white shoes, her graying dark hair was smoothly waved, her face was tanned and lightly made-up. Altogether she looked like any one of the well-groomed older women you can see sitting around the white metal tables at the club in the afternoons, discussing their dinner parties and doctors and trips to Europe. I couldn't imagine what she was doing here.

She asked me my name, and how long I'd been playing tennis. Then she demanded, "How old are you?" in that brusque way of hers.

"Thirteen."

She looked thoughtful, but all she said was, "There are a couple of good players around here. Find someone to give you a game." With which she nodded to me, and walked away.

I stood staring after her, but she seemed already to have forgotten my existence. Oh, well, some kind of a kook after all, I decided. But the way she talked, as if she really knew something about tennis. . . .

I shrugged and looked at my watch. Time to go home. I still had the living room to vacuum, and a new barbecue sauce I wanted to try with the spare ribs we were having for supper. Had Mom remembered to buy more onions? I walked past the courts toward the main gate, still thinking about supper, trying to decide if there was enough pie left for dessert tonight. Maybe, if we had ice cream with it; only I had a feeling we were out of vanilla. . . .

As I came opposite the old carriage house, I saw the woman in the blue suit talking to a man I recognized as the director of the recreation center. She seemed to be asking him something; he was shaking his head and looking puzzled and a little irritated. Maybe that's just her thing in life, I thought, asking people questions. By the time I got home, I'd almost forgotten about her.

five

THE NEXT MORNING was hot and very humid, with thunderstorms forecast for later on, but I took my tennis racket along anyway. Mrs. Morrison noticed it as I got into her station wagon, and said approvingly, "I'm glad to see you're playing more these days, Dulcie—although I don't know about today, the weather doesn't look too promising. . . . You sure you wouldn't like me to take you over to the club this afternoon? Those public courts must be pretty crowded these days, with so many people taking up tennis."

I explained about the backboard, and she nodded. "That's good practice. Still, there's nothing like a real game, or at least somebody across the net

64

hitting balls to you. If I were your parents," she added, "I'd see that you took some lessons."

But tennis lessons are expensive, I wanted to say, and in our family they're budgeted for Pat. But I didn't think Mrs. Morrison would understand. I wonder about that now. It occurs to me that she saw a lot more than she let on and was trying to help in her own way—offering me the job in the first place not only because she really needed someone but also because she'd seen how desperate I was beginning to feel at the club, tied to Eric and the pool all day. And of course she'd known my family in a casual way for several years. Mrs. Morrison may have been pretty careless about a lot of things, but she was sharp enough when it came to people.

I took the kids over to the center as usual, but halfway through the morning, while we were still at the playground, the skies turned purple, and the thunder that had been growling in the distance began to advance on us in great leaps like some big, shaggy beast. "Lions and tigers," I said to Kim, who was scared of thunderstorms, but that only made her cry harder; I'd forgotten she was scared of animals, too. A moment later a rush of wind shook out the leaves of the big trees overhead, and the first raindrops came pelting down.

I hustled the kids homeward as fast as I could, but we might as well not have hurried—the downpour caught us before we'd even reached the field,

65

and in ten seconds we were so drenched we couldn't get any wetter. I pointed this out to the kids, and Kim stopped crying to stare down at her soaked playsuit. Suddenly she giggled and spun around, holding her face up to the rain. Molly let out a whoop of joy and went skipping off across the sodden grass like a demented water sprite. Soon we were all laughing and singing and dancing around in the streaming rain, while the thunder boomed and lightning flashed pale in the distance.

When we burst in through the back door, looking like survivors of a shipwreck, clothes dripping and hair plastered to our cheeks, Mrs. Morrison exclaimed, "Good heavens!" She was addressing envelopes at the kitchen table, and looked hot and irritable.

"We've been playing in the rain!" Molly announced gleefully.

"We're all *wet!*" Kim shouted.

"Obviously," said their mother, and turned to me. "Dulcie, you should know enough to take shelter in a thunderstorm." Her tone was sharp.

"There wasn't any lightning nearby," I said apologetically. "And we were already so wet—"

"You should try it, Mommy," Molly urged. "It feels good!"

Mrs. Morrison surveyed the three of us, and then laughed. "Well, I wanted a sitter who'd do things, instead of just sitting. . . . Did you leave any rain for me? Maybe I *will* try it—I've got a headache from working in this stuffy kitchen." She stood up, glancing at Kim's beaming face, and said to me, "Hey, wouldn't it be wonderful if a certain person had actually got over her fear of S-T-O-R-M-S?"

The she kicked off her shoes and walked out the door into the teeming rain. "You're right," she called, standing there in her trim blouse and wraparound skirt. "It's glorious!"

Which was the kind of thing I liked about Mrs. Morrison.

She put my clothes in the drier and lent me an old robe, and by the time I changed back again at lunchtime, the sun had come out and the air was hotter and more sultry than ever. I was tempted to forget tennis for the day and go straight over to the pool after work; but it occurred to me that the storm would have cleared the courts for an hour or so, and even though they'd be dry by now, I might still have a chance of finding one free—provided I could hunt up someone to play with.

I was right about the courts. They'd dried off completely, and only four of the six were occupied, although it wouldn't be long before more players arrived to fill them. I glanced around hopefully for someone I could challenge to a set or two—two was the limit if other people were waiting to play—but didn't see anyone who seemed to be looking for a game. I did notice Mark Leonard lounging on a bench over by the water fountain in his tennis clothes, looking bored and superior as usual, but it would never have occurred to me to approach him. I knew him by reputation as one of the better high school players, though he didn't compete much in club tournaments, and I'd never seen him play. The word was that his girl friends took up more time than his tennis these days, anyway.

Nora Krebs was finishing up a set of doubles with three other girls on the second court. I decided to wait and see if she wanted to play some singles later on. Nora's older than I am, but kind of fat and slow; still she'd be better than nothing. So I waited until they came off the court, but when I asked her, Nora said, "Oh, Dulcie, it's much too hot, I'm ready to *melt*," and went off giggling with the others to the water fountain, hoping Mark Leonard would notice them.

I walked slowly along the path toward the backboard, thinking I should have taken Mrs. Morrison up on her offer to drive me to the club. Maybe I didn't like the place much, but at least I could be pretty sure of finding a game there. Oh, well, I'd hit against the backboard for a while, and then go have a swim and see my friends and stop making such a big deal about tennis. . . .

The earnest little tow-headed boy was at the backboard again, working on the forehand I'd taught him. I waved as he turned to chase a ball, and he called, "Hey! That lady was looking for you!"

"What lady?"

"You know, that same lady that was here before."

I looked around, didn't see anyone, shrugged, and unzipped my racket cover. I began hitting backhands against the board, hard and rather mechanically, trying to remember how long it would be before my friend Amy got home from camp. Amy and I always had a lot of fun playing tennis together, even if we did tend to fool around a lot and break up whenever we got into a long rally. This was only the middle of July, though, it'd be another month at least—

A voice behind me said, "Knees, Dulcie."

I whirled around. She wasn't wearing blue today, but a yellow shirt and white slacks. The dark glasses were the same, and the air of authority—which I guess is why I didn't even smile at someone's suddenly saying "Knees" to me that way, out of thin air.

"You weren't getting down to the ball," she explained. "Bend your knees and drop that left shoulder more."

She stood watching, hands on hips, as I hit a few more backhands, concentrating this time, and then said in her abrupt way: "I've arranged some singles for you. Unfortunately it's not possible to arrange for a court as well—heaven knows why they don't have some sort of system here—but if we hurry . . ." She nodded at the empty sixth court nearby.

I stared at her, and my glance must have gone

automatically to her feet—she was wearing fashionable platform sandals—because she gave a short laugh and said, "Oh, I'm not your opponent, Dulcie, never fear. . . . No, I've found a boy who's not a bad player, at least whenever he chooses to exert himself. He ought to be able to give you a game, at any rate. Come along."

I followed her obediently over to the court and opened the gate, standing back to let her precede me. "No," she said, "I'll watch from outside. I'm purely a spectator—on this occasion, anyway. . . . Now where is that boy?" She looked around impatiently. "Well, you'd better get onto the court before someone else grabs it. My name is Mrs. Trask, by the way," she said, and held out her hand formally.

We shook hands—her grip was hard and firm—and I went on through the gate, feeling more bewildered than ever. Mrs. Trask . . . the name meant nothing to me; and who was this mysterious opponent she'd found for me? I stood at the baseline, bouncing a ball self-consciously, and then the gate on the other side clanked open, and in came Mark Leonard—dark hair, slouch, and all. I swallowed hard. Give me a game . . . oh, sure!

As for Mark, he made no effort to hide his disgust at the sight of me—a girl, and just a kid at that, three or four years younger than himself. He shot a furious glance at Mrs. Trask, who had seated herself on a bench outside the enclosure, and who returned his look calmly—at least as far as you could read her expression behind the dark glasses.

"You Dulcie Kane?" he said roughly, coming forward to toss a towel over the net post.

"Yes."

"Any relation to Pat?"

"She's my sister."

"She's not a bad player," he observed, in a tone that said clearly he could beat Pat any day of the week and would certainly make short work of her little sister. A boring prospect—he'd get it over with as quickly as possible. He walked back to the baseline and, without even looking at me to see if I was ready, fired his first warm-up ball at me. It took me by surprise, and I hit it into the net. Next he hit a vicious backhand hard into the corner, which I didn't even reach for.

"Sorry," he called mockingly. "Didn't realize you were a lefty."

Maybe not; but he certainly knew well enough that the point of a warm-up is to hit the ball to your opponent, not past him. I retrieved the ball from the corner and very deliberately sent it straight to his forehand, so that he didn't even have to take a step. He slammed it back at me, but I'd begun to take his measure, and returned it almost as hard.

This surprised him. He mis-hit the ball into the net, and then stood inspecting the handle of his racket as though something had interfered with his grip.

Then he shrugged, whammed another ball at me—but to me this time—and we exchanged ground strokes for a while in a fairly normal fashion, though I couldn't resist trying a couple of cross-court shots to his backhand to make him run. He was fast, I could see that, and strong; but when he came to the net to volley the easy balls I put up for him, he tended to overhit the ball—and most of his overheads went into the net.

When I came up to take my own practice volleys, I could see what he was thinking: what a waste of time, she'll never come to the net anyway, girls never do, they're scared of it. As if to dispose of this point right away, he began by hitting the ball hard and low, straight at me. I sent the first couple into the net, but as I've said, I love to volley, and on this score at least I wasn't going to be intimidated. Forehand, backhand, overhead—I kept smacking the ball back down at his feet, until finally he tried some passing shots, but I got most of those too.

"Hey, not bad," he said at last and gave me this big smile that's supposed to make all the girls flip; but it didn't do anything for me. Obviously he'd decided to patronize me, just in case I managed to win a few points from him. "You could give your big sister lessons at the net."

And maybe I'll give you some, too, I thought grimly, as he spun his racket for the serve. I called out, "Smooth." Smooth it was; and suddenly I felt nervous again. In the fun of warming up, proving I could trade shots with this conceited character—and it was fun, in a peculiar way—I'd forgotten all about my horrible serve. I thought of saying I'd take side instead, so that Mark would serve first, but that would have sounded completely moronic: not only was there no wind, there was hardly a breath of air stirring in that sticky heat, and the sun wasn't bright enough to be a problem, being just a brassy haze in the sky.

No way, Dulcie, I told myself. Unfortunately there's just no way you can play tennis without serving, sooner or later—and it might as well be sooner.

So I served, and lost the first game in straight points. I didn't even double fault; it was simply that my serve had nothing on it and was often short besides. Mark just kept putting it away, brutally and methodically. The only return I got to was a backhand I couldn't handle except with a lob, another weak part of my game, and in my effort to get the ball over Mark's head, I hit it out by a good three feet.

I kept my head down as we changed sides, not wanting to look over at Mrs. Trask, who must surely be regretting her interest in me already. After all, she'd gone to the trouble of arranging a game for me, and even if it turned out to be a mismatch against a stronger player, her choice of Mark was a compliment in itself.

I got into position quickly; but Mark had reverted to his earlier bored manner, sauntering casually back to the baseline and taking his time about getting ready to serve. I looked over at him, feeling small and inadequate and immature—and realized suddenly that that was exactly what he meant me to feel.

All right, Dulcie, I ordered myself: you're going to get his serve back, no matter how hard he hits it, and the next ball, and the one after that. Whatever happens, it'll be good experience, and it's certainly a lot better than playing pat-ball with Nora Krebs.

But I hardly saw Mark's first serve, which came whipping down the center line so fast it left me flat-footed. In fact I wasn't sure the ball was in; but Mark seemed to assume it had been, so I said nothing and moved over to the other court. This time he served wide, to my forehand—either he'd forgotten I was left-handed or didn't think it mattered—and I didn't try for the ball because it was clearly out, five or six inches into the alley.

Automatically I moved up a foot or so to receive the second serve, though for all I knew, he'd hit it as hard as his first, and saw to my astonishment that Mark had moved across to serve into the deuce court again. He glanced over at me impatiently.

I said, "Sorry, but that was out."

"It looked good to me."

"It bounced in the alley."

"I thought it caught the line."

We glared at each other. Of course on a hard-surface court there's no chalk to kick up and no tell-tale print left by the ball. I glanced at Mrs. Trask, but she was watching us impassively. If he wasn't going to appeal to her, I certainly wasn't though she must surely have seen that the serve was out.

"Thirty–love," Mark said. "Come on, move!"

"No," I said. "It's still fifteen–love. You can take your first serve over if you want."

I felt shaky, and surprised at myself—listen to Dulcie making waves!—but determined to hold my ground.

"Well, well," Mark sneered. "Who are you supposed to be, anyway—Billie Jean King? And that makes me Bobby Riggs?" He strode back into his original position. "You want a nice polite little serve —okay, here it is."

He popped a soft little blooper over the net. I hit it hard down the line; he made no move for it. "Point to you," he drawled. "So now it's fifteen–all, what do you know? Wow, the kid's really pressing me."

I said as calmly as I could, "I like a hard serve, thanks anyway."

"Oh, you do, do you? I thought maybe you wanted me to behave like a little gentleman. Well, now we know where we stand," Mark said, and fired his serve at me with all his strength.

This time I got my racket on it and blocked it back cross-court. But he'd come up to the net fast and volleyed the ball deep to my forehand. I probably should have tried a passing shot, but I was a little off-balance and put up a lob instead—too short this time. (I've got to work on my lobs! I told myself furiously.) Mark backed up to take the overhead with a leisurely ho-hum air. He had the whole court for his smash, and he put it in the net.

Neither of us made any comment. Now it was 15–30. Mark served wide again to my forehand, not following it up to the net this time, and I got off my good return into his backhand corner. His turn to be caught off-balance—I'd already noticed his backhand wasn't terribly strong or consistent—and to try a desperation lob. It was high, but not too deep; I let it bounce midway between the service line and the baseline, smacked a short cross-court shot to his backhand again, and came to the net. Mark had stayed back, anticipating a down-the-line shot to his forehand, but he charged the ball and tried a passing shot off my backhand. I was ready for that, and volleyed it away for the point: 15–40.

Now Mark decided to change tactics on his serve and keep the ball away from my forehand. But although his serve had a lot of power and a fair amount of spin, he really didn't have much control; and as I'd suspected, no second serve to speak of, just a slower version of the first. His first serve to my backhand was so wild that even he couldn't dispute my call of "Out!" (I'd begun calling every shot on my side, not to be nasty, just in self-defense.) His second serve went into the net.

My game. And now my serve again, and history repeating itself. I just couldn't get the ball in deep or hard, and although I did manage this time to get my racket on some of Mark's returns, I was on the defensive and usually too far out of position to hit a decent shot. Game to him; I'd won just one point.

As we changed sides, Mrs. Trask rose and came over to the fence. "Mark," she said, "stop trying to murder your serve. And Dulcie, just keep getting the ball back for now. Force him to make the errors."

With which she returned to her bench.

"Well, she's impartial, anyway," Mark growled. "Whoever she thinks she is." I'd been hoping he knew something about her; but before I could ask him anything, he'd stalked away over to his side of the net.

Again I broke Mark's serve, if you can put it that way. He was still aiming for my backhand, which produced two more double faults. When he finally did get a first serve in, I was more than ready for it, and hit it down the line for a winner. I couldn't help smiling at his look of outrage, and I thought I heard Mrs. Trask give a dry chuckle from the sidelines. Thereafter he stopped trying to place his serve, just hitting it hard—not paying much attention to Mrs. Trask's advice, as far as I could see—and charging the net after it. I stayed back, remembering what she'd said, and hit my returns as solidly as I could, passing him at the net whenever possible, but mainly retrieving, scrambling all over the court after the ball, sending it back and back and back until, sure enough, he'd miss a smash, or volley the ball out.

As thunder rumbled again in the distance and the air thickened and clung to us like a second skin, the score went to 3–all, then 3–4 as I lost my serve for the fourth time. And now Mark really bore down —obviously furious at having lost his serve three times in succession, but forcing himself to concentrate. He blew two aces by me, his volleys were hard and accurate for a change, and in no time at all he'd won a love game, and I was serving again at 3–5.

I wiped my sweaty hand on my shorts, took a firm grip on my racket, and hit another of those hopeless wobbly serves. Mark, who'd taken to standing about three feet behind the service line, was instantly on top of it and slammed it deep to my forehand corner. A sure put-away, but I raced across for it anyway —retrieve, retrieve—and scooped up a lob I was sure was going out.

Miraculously (or maybe just because the air was so heavy) the ball bounced a few inches inside the baseline; but Mark had stayed with it, and now he ran around the ball to take it with his forehand, hitting another hard drive to my backhand and rushing the net after it. But I'd had plenty of time to get back in position, and passed him with my best shot of the afternoon—a low cross-court shot with plenty of top-spin on it that just skimmed the net, sinking as it went, and bounced away at an impossible angle.

"Nice shot," Mark said, to my amazement. He waved his racket and called, "Hey, you dig that backhand? She's pulling a Rosewall on me!"

For the first time I realized that we had a gallery of sorts—some friends of Mark's who'd wandered over to enjoy the spectacle of Mark demolishing some junior high school girl. So now he was playing to them, I thought angrily; and of course he could afford to act the nice guy now, with only a few points remaining between him and the set.

I looked over at Mrs. Trask, as impassive as ever behind her dark glasses, and saw that she'd been joined on the bench by my tow-headed friend, who looked anything but neutral. "Hey, Dulcie, you can still beat him!" he yelled, as I walked over to the advantage court to serve again. Mark's friends hooted with laughter, and I smiled and shook my head; but I felt oddly cheered.

Trying to get some depth into my serve, I hit the first one out. My second serve was so cautious— please don't let me double-fault, I was praying—that Mark simply dumped a drop shot over the net, and I was back where I'd started. Or not quite: at least the score was 15–all instead of love–30.

I got ready to serve again, tossed the ball too high, and caught it.

"Hey, she's sort of a doll," remarked one of Mark's friends, leaning up against the fence. "Look at all that pretty blonde hair. Another Chris Evert, I don't think." They all thought that was very funny. I bit my lip, trying to shut them out. Suddenly all I wanted to do was get this game over with, win or lose. I remembered what my doubles partner Sam had said—"Just get the ball in play"—and without bothering to take any backswing at all, I tossed the ball up quickly and it hit flat and low over the net—and hard too, harder than I'd meant to, because I was mad. I was sure the serve was going out, but instead the ball skidded into the corner and shot off into the alley past Mark, who just looked at it in surprise.

Cheers and clapping and cries of "Ace, Ace!" from his friends, which at least disposed of any idea he might have had of disputing the call.

My face burned—I knew it was a dumb-looking serve—but I reminded myself that the score was now 30–15, the first time in the entire set that I'd gone ahead on my serve. So I did it again: hit the ball flat and low, consciously aiming for the outside corner this time because it was Mark's backhand. He was still standing up close to receive, obviously considering the last serve a fluke (well, so did I, for that matter), and had to backpedal fast to reach the ball at all. Still he hit a fairly good cross-court shot at such an angle it might have gone for a winner—except that the momentum of my serve had carried me forward, and I got to the ball in time to hit a forehand down the side of the court where Mark wasn't. Again remembering Sam, I didn't even hit it hard, just carefully—40–15.

The next point really should have been Mark's. My new serve, if that's what it was, went into the net the first time—I was hitting it so low, I'd just been lucky so far—and my second was just an indecisive dink. But Mark had moved back to receive this time and had to dive for the ball. Somehow he got his racket on it, but stumbled as he hit it, and the ball hit the tape, wavered a moment, and fell back onto his side of the court.

"Hey, she really psyched you out of that one," crowed one of his friends as we changed courts. Someone else called, "What's your score now, hotshot?"

"Five–four," Mark said tersely.

"Never mind," yelled another, "you're going to be rained out in a minute anyway."

"Yeah, maybe you'd better play it safe, Leonard —give the little girl a rain check."

I'd been too intent on the game to pay much attention to the weather. Now I noticed that although there was still a pale glare of sunshine on the court and the heat was as intense as ever, clouds were piling up overhead and the thunder had grown much louder. As I took my position on the court to receive serve, I felt a few scattered drops of rain and thought, Oh, no, let's play this one game at least. He's going to blast his serve right by me, probably, but at least let's finish the set.

We did, and Mark won it then and there, 6–4, but it was the best tennis we'd played all afternoon, with raindrops speckling the surface of the court and the lightning flaring around us. Mark's friends complained it was going to pour at any minute, but they stayed to watch. Mark did ace me, twice—but twice I got off good deep returns on his second serve, and recklessly followed them into the net; and for the first time we had a quick sharp exchange of volleys that got some honest applause from the gallery—and even a reluctant grin from Mark as I put the ball past him for the second time.

At 30–all, Mark missed his first serve and elected to stay back on his second, and we got hung up on one of those incredibly long backcourt rallies—the kind that begin to seem almost funny after a while, so that you lose your concentration and wind up hitting the ball out or into the net for no good reason. But we were both holding on for dear life, the rain blowing in our faces now as we drove the ball back and forth, forehand, backhand, forehand, backhand—keeping the ball deep, but also trying to edge each other just slightly out of position, working for the crucial opening.

I'd been hitting ball after ball to Mark's forehand, trying to maneuver him off-center, but a couple of strides of his long legs always got him back in position. Then, little by little, I shortened my stroke, forcing him forward, at the same time angling the ball more and more towards the alley. At last, I thought I had him where I wanted him, and charged his next shot to whip the ball cross-court, a backhand he couldn't possibly get to—which he didn't, but it didn't matter. In my eagerness, I'd hit the ball out. Forty-thirty, and set point. I was disgusted with myself. Let him make the errors, Mrs. Trask had said, and she was right. I knew Mark's ground strokes weren't as steady as mine, and if I'd only been content to go on trading shots, I probably would have won the point sooner or later on sheer endurance. Instead I had to try for a winner. Well, I wouldn't make that mistake any more. Somehow I'd get the score to deuce, and then just wear him down.

I wiped the rain out of my face and crouched tensely for Mark's serve. His first one hit the net tape so hard it almost broke it—an ace for sure, if it had gone over. The second serve didn't have much on it —Mark was being cautious for a change—and in turn I returned it cautiously, afraid of hitting it out. He took the ball on the rise, slapping it back at me and charging the net. Okay, I thought: let him make the error. And I lifted a short lob, watched him back up for it—racket poised behind his head—waited for him to smash it into the net, as he'd done with almost every overhead so far, and saw him slam the ball like a bullet into my backhand corner for the point, game, and set.

Mark's friends cheered; but he stood resting his racket on top of the net, and said, "Hey, you sure that was in?"

I looked at his face to see if he was putting me on, but he was in earnest. It was the nearest he came to apologizing for his earlier behavior.

"On the line," I told him. "A perfect shot."

We shook hands across the net, and he gave me a pat on the shoulder. "You're a real little scrapper, you know, Dulcie? You had me worried there for a while."

I just smiled and said, "I wish we could play another set."

He groaned, pretending exhaustion. "Sure you do. Taking advantage of us old folks. Well, keep it up, kiddo, and I'll see you around—like maybe at Forest Hills someday. You better tell your sister to move over."

He slung his wet towel around his neck, waved, and loped off through the rain that was falling quite heavily now; and so we parted friends, more or less —though I wonder what he would have said if I'd beaten him?

six

I FOUND MYSELF alone on the court. Everyone else had taken shelter from the storm. I looked around for my racket cover, and realized I'd left it over by the backboard. My racket had nylon strings, but even so, I hurried off the court, clutching it under my arm, as a great clap of thunder sounded directly overhead and the rain came down in a solid sheet. For the second time that day I was completely drenched, but this time I didn't feel like dancing or singing. I was brooding over my useless serve and all the mistakes I'd made, and wondering how I would have done if we'd been able to play another set.

As I squelched over to where I thought I'd left my gear, I heard a voice calling my name over the noise of the storm. I peered through the rain and saw Mrs. Trask standing just inside the small tennis shack that stood opposite the middle courts. She was holding up my racket cover and shoulder bag and beckoning to me impatiently.

"Good heavens," she said, as I arrived on the run. "Just look at you! Don't you have a sweater or something to put on?"

I shook my head. "I'm healthy, though, I never catch cold."

"Well, let's hope not." She studied me for a moment. "You're really not the least bit tired, are you, Dulcie? I never saw you look out of breath out there, or even get particularly sweaty."

She'd taken my racket from me and was rubbing it dry with a towel—though I thought maybe I could have used the towel more. Now she hefted the racket in her hand and said absently, "You really ought to have something a little lighter . . . and gut, of course, not nylon." It was an old racket of Pat's, but I didn't mention that. "It's important, you know, more important than most people realize," Mrs. Trask went on, and I thought she was still talking about tennis rackets; but she said seriously, "Anyone who can play in this kind of sticky heat and not be affected by it . . . why, the East Coast probably has the worst climate in the world for tennis. If you can play well here. . . ."

She looked at me and laughed, a real laugh this time. "Not that it's all that hot at the moment, is it?

You're actually shivering, and no wonder. Come on, Dulcie, I've got a sweater in my car, and anyway I want to talk to you."

Somehow you didn't argue with Mrs. Trask; or at least I didn't then. I've learned to since, about important things, anyway—meaning things to do with tennis, of course. In fact she's urged me to speak up whenever I disagree with her, saying that no automaton ever played good tennis.

Anyhow, although I knew I ought to be getting home, rain or no rain, I waited while she tied a plastic scarf over her hair and then followed her through the downpour to the parking lot. I saw her shy involuntarily at a bolt of lightning, and thought, why, she's afraid of thunderstorms, just like Kim. But it was hard to imagine the same cure working with Mrs. Trask.

Her car was a gray Mercedes with light blue upholstery. I felt awkward about my wet clothes, but she made an impatient motion for me to get in, handed me an immaculate white cashmere sweater from the back seat, and sat back herself, lighting a cigarette.

"Don't you ever smoke, Dulcie," she said, glancing over at me sharply. "I never did until. . . . Well, never mind, just don't ever take it up." She rolled down her window a few inches to let the smoke out and sat gazing thoughtfully over the wet expanse of the parking lot, almost deserted now in the drumming rain. I wondered why she didn't remove the dark glasses. Certainly it was murky enough outside, except for occassional flares of lightning, and the windshield glass was heavily tinted.

"So," she said, turning back to me. "Why didn't you beat him?"

I'm sure my mouth fell open; at any rate, it was a moment before I could stammer, "But, my gosh, Mrs. Trask. He's older than me, and stronger, and . . ."

"Never mind all that. Why didn't you beat him?"

I huddled the soft white sweater more closely around my shoulders and then looked at her intent face, and the anger I'd felt for a moment drained away. "My serve," I said.

"Yes, your serve. Except for that one game, and we'll come back to that later. What else?"

"I can't lob. At least, sometimes I can, but . . ." I thought of that last point, and bit my lip. "I guess that was a stupid thing to try, there at the end. I could probably have got the ball past him—"

"No, I'm not so sure. And he really can't hit his overhead, so it was a good percentage shot on your part. Just remember, the percentages don't always work, and don't let it get you down. But I agree you need lots of work on your lobs, especially the backhand. You've got a good, strong, flexible wrist, and that ought to be one of your best shots."

She looked at me quizzically, waiting for me to go on.

"Well, volleying, getting up to the net. I mean, I know you told me to stay back . . ."

"That's not quite what I said, but never mind. I wanted to see how well you could play a defensive game, even though it's obviously not your natural style. But all right. What about your volleying?"

"It's what I love to do," I told her earnestly. "And I know I'm good at it, I could win lots of points at the net if I could only *get* there. But I hardly ever can."

"Ah," Mrs. Trask said, and smiled to herself. "Right on, as you kids say. How and when to approach the net—that's something we'll be working on. But tell me one more thing, Dulcie," she went on, before I could ask what she meant. "Didn't you think Mark should have let up on you a little—on his serve, at least? After all, he was playing a girl, and as you said, he's older and stronger. He didn't have to keep trying to blast you off the court."

"No!" I said, more loudly than I'd intended. "I just meant he had all those things going for him. But if he'd let up on me, well, that would *really* have made me mad! I mean, I was mad anyway about the way he tried to psych me out when we were warming up— and then that serve that was out by a mile, and he *knew* it. . . ."

I stopped and glanced uncertainly at Mrs. Trask, who said calmly, "And why didn't I say something, is that what you're wondering? Well, Dulcie, I wanted to see how you'd handle it. You stuck to your guns, and that's what I needed to know. If you'd been meek and polite about it . . ." She shrugged and tossed away her cigarette. "Also, you made your anger work for you; you didn't lose control. And that's more important than you can possibly imagine, especially when you get into serious competition, with all the pressure that involves."

She turned in her seat to face me directly. "All right, Dulcie. When can you start?"

"Start?"

"I want to give you some coaching. I've seen enough now to be sure." She must have misinterpreted my blank look, because she smiled wryly and said, "If you're wondering about my qualifications—well, I used to be a pretty good player myself, though I doubt if you'd heard of me. That was back in the Dark Ages, of course. And I've run tennis clinics in various places we've lived—my husband's had to move around a lot—as well as teaching my own children to play. . . ."

I tried not to show my surprise. Somehow it was hard to think of Mrs. Trask in connection with a home and family. And as for her tennis career—well, I'd heard my parents talk about the top players of the past, and her name didn't mean anything to me. But of course Trask would be her married name, I realized.

"At any rate," she was continuing, "I'd thought of starting up another clinic here—we've just moved here recently—and then I spotted you. You're a natural, Dulcie, in the way you move and attack the ball, and in your court sense, as I saw today; and players like that don't come along very often. Of course, none of that means a thing without hard work and dedication and—well, a lot of other things you still have to find out about yourself."

For a moment her face looked tired and almost sad. But when she spoke again, it was in her normal brisk voice. "Understand, Dulcie, I'm not offering to coach you just out of the goodness of my heart. It's a challenge to me as well. In fact it's what every teacher hopes for—the chance to work with a really promising young player, to help her make the most of her natural ability . . . and a left-handed player at that, in your case. I'm left-handed, too."

She smiled at me. Like Mrs. Morrison, she seemed to assume that everything was all settled.

I said rather wildly, "But Mrs. Trask—you mean you think I could be really *good*? A really good tennis player? Like—well, like a *pro* someday?"

"Well, that's up to you isn't it? But I think you have the basic ability, yes. I wouldn't be spending my time on you otherwise."

The rain was stopping. I rolled down my window and took a couple of breaths of fresh, damp air. The whole idea was so new to me that I couldn't think about it calmly. I felt excited and confused and upset all at once, and a whole swarm of objections filled my mind. I blurted out the simplest of them: "But how much would the lessons cost? I mean, we don't have a whole lot of money, and besides . . ."

"Oh for heaven's sake, child!" Mrs. Trask sounded exasperated. "Don't you understand? You're not investing in me, I'm investing in you. If I decide in a week's time—or in a year, for that matter—that you just haven't got what it takes, why, I'll tell you so, and that will be that. In the meantime"—she rapped the steering wheel with her knuckles for emphasis—"I'll expect you to work very hard indeed. I want you to be quite clear about that, Dulcie. You'll have to work harder than you've ever worked at anything in your life. I'm not talking about a few lessons, you see, I'm talking about *coaching.* That means you'll be spending three or four hours every day just hitting a tennis ball."

"Three or four hours!" I echoed. "But Mrs. Trask, I have a job in the mornings, and—"

"Well, then, we'll work in the afternoons. Not here"—she gestured dismissively at the courts behind us, already beginning to steam again in the sun—"partly because of the difficulty of reserving a court, and partly because I'd rather have you play on a composition surface. We don't have a court, but our next door neighbors do. I can arrange to have it at a regular time, so that's no problem. As for practice partners . . . well, we'll be doing mostly drill at first, of course, and I can handle that. . . ."

She frowned, thinking aloud, while I sat feeling stunned. "I'll want you to play an actual set from time to time. Later on you'll need a regular practice partner, but for now—well, my husband can help on weekends, and the older Carter boy . . . yes, and my daughter Kate will be here in August for a few weeks. I'd rather have you play against men for now," she explained, "but Kate hits a good hard ball, even if she isn't terribly consistent, so—"

"But Mrs. Trask—!"

"But what?" She turned to look at me, and I felt she was really seeing me for the first time from behind those big dark glasses of hers. "This is a wonderful opportunity for you, Dulcie, if I do say so. Don't you want it? Perhaps I've misjudged you, after all." Her tone was suddenly chilly.

"No, it's not that! It's partly . . . well, you see, I've never even thought about tennis *seriously*, the way you mean. I mean, I like to play, but I don't know how I'd feel about spending so much time at it."

"Well, the only way to find out is to try it," she said reasonably, and added with a sudden smile, "I'm sorry, Dulcie. I've been rushing you, haven't I? It's a habit of mine whenever I get enthusiastic about something. And of course if no one's ever told you how good you could be. . . ." She shrugged. "As far as the work goes—well, I have the feeling you're a worker at heart, Dulcie. The kind who keeps plugging away at something until you get it right. Isn't that true?"

I nodded dumbly. Of course it wasn't the work I was worried about, anyway, even the amount of time involved; it was the whole rest of my life.

"And that's the iceberg," Mrs. Trask was saying. "The part you don't see when you watch a top player in competition. Behind every good forehand he hits, there are—oh, a hundred thousand forehands he's hit in practice, good, bad, and indifferent. And thousands of hours of just plain dogged, hard work. Which means going out and playing in all kinds of weather, and never mind if you're in the mood or not. In fact, there'll be days when you'll feel sick at the very sight of a tennis ball and wish you'd taken up chess or modern dance instead. The point is, there aren't any instant prodigies in tennis. The talent has to be there in the first place, but that's really the least of it."

She saw I wasn't really listening and said in a gentler voice: "What is it, Dulcie? What's the real problem?"

"It's just—well, it's a lot to think about, all at once. And my family—my parents, and my sister ..." My voice trailed away. I was trying to imagine just what their reaction *would* be to all of this. Disbelief, to begin with; and then. ...

Mrs. Trask looked puzzled. "Well, I don't see what your sister has to do with it, but as far as your parents are concerned, naturally I'll want to talk to them as soon as possible. It's important for them to understand just what's involved and, of course, if they don't play tennis themselves or know much about it—"

"Oh, they love tennis," I told her unhappily; after all, wasn't that the whole problem? "They play every chance they get and watch the matches on TV and go to Forest Hills every year."

"Well, then—"

"It's partly a matter of time, Mrs. Trask, really it is. I mean, I have this job in the mornings, like I said, and both my parents work, so I have a lot of stuff to do at home. Taking care of the house and cooking, and all that. I mean, I just wouldn't have three hours to play tennis every day."

"This sister of yours, is she older or younger?" Mrs. Trask was leaning back in the corner with her arms folded, watching me.

"Older."

"Well, why can't she help out around the house? What does she do with herself all day long?"

"She—she plays tennis," I said, and had to smile in spite of myself when Mrs. Trask burst out laughing.

"You make it sound so tragic!" she said. "Is she that bad?"

"Oh, no. I mean, she's quite good."

"Not as good as you are, though, I'm willing to bet. Or will be. . . . But surely, Dulcie, when your parents hear about this chance of yours, they'll arrange to take some of the household chores off your hands. After all, a tennis-playing family—I should think they'd all be delighted for you. Including your older sister."

I must have looked as doubtful as I felt, because she said, "No? But why on earth not?"

I shook my head. As I said before, how do you go about explaining your family to someone else? I didn't want to complain or sound disloyal. And Mrs. Trask still scared me a little, she was so uncompromising about anything that stood in her way. I was afraid she'd just dismiss my reservations as being too trivial to worry about.

She said with a sigh, "Well, all right, Dulcie. How about two hours, then? Do you think you could manage that?"

I calculated rapidly. If I could get to Mrs. Trask's house—or her neighbors'—right after work, I could put in two hours on the tennis court and still be home at my usual hour. And my family would assume I'd spent the time here at the recreation center the way I'd been doing. Not that any one ever really checked up on me, anyway.

I said carefully, "Yes, I think I could do that. I'd have to be home by three, though. Or three-thirty at the latest."

Mrs. Trask laughed. "And what happens if you aren't—do you turn into a pumpkin or something? You sound just like Cinderella." At the look on my face, she said quickly, "Well, all right, Dulcie, I guess I'll have to settle for that—at first, anyway. Now, where is it you work, and what time can I pick you up?"

"Well . . ." If Mrs. Morrison knew about Mrs. Trask, I thought, it wouldn't be long before my parents did. "I could meet you here at the center," I said. "I mean, it isn't far away, it's just a baby-sitting job, and I can easily walk over from there, and . . ."

"And what?" Mrs. Trask said sharply. "Dulcie, people are going to have to know about this sooner or later, especially your parents. I'm not trying to kidnap you, for heaven's sake! In fact," she said decisively, taking her car keys out of her bag, "I think it would be a good idea if I drove you home and talked to your parents right now."

"They're not home now," I said desperately.

"Well, then, I'll call them tonight. In the meantime, I can at least give you a ride home, can't I?" She put the key in the ignition.

But Pat might be home by now, I thought. What with the thunderstorm, she and Eric might have left the club early—and how would I explain Mrs. Trask and the Mercedes? I'm no good at lying, especially to Pat. I said, "Please, Mrs. Trask, thanks a lot, but I'd just as soon walk. I mean, I like to walk, anyway, and . . ." I looked at my watch. "Gosh! I'd really better get going."

I opened the car door, and then remembered the sweater. I folded it carefully and leaned over to put it on the back seat.

"Dulcie, Dulcie." Mrs. Trask shook her head at me, smiling a little. "So aggressive on the tennis court

—yes, you are, you know, that's what made my mind up about you—and so meek and mild off it. You're going to have to change that, I'm afraid, if you're ever going to play first-rate tennis. Nice guys finish last, as I think some baseball player said."

"Leo Durocher," I said automatically. My father's a baseball fan as well as a tennis nut. I gathered up my gear and slid out of the car into the sunlight, knowing I had to find some way of explaining things to Mrs. Trask.

"Mrs. Trask," I began, running my thumb over the worn handle of my tennis racket—Pat's tennis racket—"I really appreciate your offering to coach me, and . . . well, everything you've said. And I want to do it, really I do, and I'll work just as hard as you want me to. But—do we have to tell my parents right away? Couldn't we just get started and see how things go?"

She started to say something, but I went on earnestly, "I mean, maybe I won't last more than a couple of days, after all; or you'll change your mind about me, the way you said you might. And then, well, it would all be just a big fuss over nothing. But if everything goes okay, and I'm making progress, and we both want to go on with it—well, wouldn't that be time enough to talk to my parents?"

Her face was impassive again behind the heavy glasses. At last she said, "All right, Dulcie. It's against my better judgement, but all right. Maybe when we get to know each other better you can tell me what this is all about. In the meantime,"—she started the car—"what time shall I pick you up tomorrow?"

"Tomorrow?"

"Why not? No time like the present. We've only got about six weeks until school starts," she said seriously. "And now you'd better get going on that walk of yours. It's a good thing you like to walk, by the way, because you'll be doing a lot of it eventually— walking and jogging and skipping rope and a whole lot of other things you never thought had anything to do with tennis. Oh, I can see you're as strong as a little pony," she said, at my look of surprise, "but the younger you start in on some serious conditioning, the better. See you tomorrow, then."

She gave her characteristic abrupt nod and started to pull away; then she slowed and called over the purr of the engine, "Oh, Dulcie—you never told me what time."

"One o'clock," I called back. "Or maybe a few minutes after. Five after, say."

"Five minutes after one," she repeated, with a smile at my precision. "All right, I'll be here."

I watched the gray Mercedes turn out of the parking lot, Mrs. Trask sitting forward at the wheel as if she had to concentrate hard on seeing the road before her. Of course, I thought, there's something wrong with her vision, that's why the dark glasses; special glasses, probably. And maybe that's why she had to give up playing tennis. How sad, if she was really good. I wondered if by tomorrow I could get up the nerve to ask her what her maiden name had been, and what titles she'd won and against whom.

Tomorrow! I started off toward home, my stomach churning in a kind of delayed reaction. What if I wasn't as good as Mrs. Trask thought? Well, good wasn't the word, not yet; I knew I was just a beginner when it came to serious tennis. But what if I didn't have the potential she seemed to see in me?

I remembered a music teacher of Pat's years ago, who'd decided Pat had it in her to become a good violinist; and how Pat had struggled for two years with that stubborn, squeaky fiddle, until the teacher finally admitted regretfully that she just didn't have the ear for it or the temperament or the hands (whatever that all meant; Pat took up the piano soon afterwards.) My father was furious at the teacher, who he said had just been indulging in wishful thinking all along, and Pat wound up hating the very sound of the violin. Well, I didn't think I could ever hate playing tennis, and Mrs. Trask certainly didn't strike me as the wishful-thinking type, but still. . . .

The second thunderstorm seemed to have cleared the air at last. The sun shone brightly from a polished blue sky, and there was a good smell of fresh-cut grass from somebody's lawn as I went by. My sneakers were still damp, and after a while I took them off, tied the laces together, slung them over my shoulder, and padded home barefoot through the brilliant summer afternoon—thinking not about meat loaf for supper or Dad's shirts that needed ironing, but about what a dumb-sounding name Dulcie Kane would be for a champion tennis player.

seven

IT'S FUNNY, the things you can get nervous about. That first morning I found myself worrying about the kind of house the Trasks lived in, and what their neighbors were like—the ones with the private tennis court. I thought of the big, formal places in the Greenhaven section of town, some of which still came equipped with maids and gardeners as well as swimming pools and tennis courts and billiard rooms and I don't know what else. I wished I could have worn my one tennis dress, or at least a white shirt and shorts; but I knew Mrs. Morrison would raise her eyebrows at that, and certainly a white outfit was hardly the most practical costume for grubbing around in the playground with the kids.

For Pete's sake, Dulcie, I kept telling myself, you're not going to tea, you're just going to hit a tennis ball, and Mrs. Trask won't care how you're dressed. Still, I couldn't help wishing I looked more businesslike somehow—more like a real tennis player. To make matters worse, at lunchtime Kim overturned her glass of chocolate milk—it would be chocolate— and most of it went into my lap. I stood in the kitchen dabbing frantically at my old green-plaid shorts, glad that Mrs. Morrison was still out somewhere, and wondered if I could smuggle a change of clothes along with me from now on. Rolled up in my towel with my bathing suit, maybe? Oh sure, nothing like a wrinkled wet tennis dress to impress the butler!

But I needn't have worried, it wasn't that kind of scene at all. The Trask's house turned out to be a converted barn way out on the edge of town, in what had once been farming country; and the next-door neighbors' place—their name was Carter—was the old farmhouse the barn had once belonged to. The tennis court stood in the middle of a field, a long gray green rectangle open to the sun and wind, with a weather-beaten bench just inside the gate and a court roller propped in a corner. The Carters' old horse Sally often grazed nearby, and there were usually a couple of dogs nosing about in the field for rabbit holes or forgotten bones.

As for lawns and formal gardens . . . well, to get to the court, you crossed the wide farm driveway, ducked under a ramshackle grape arbor, skirted a noisy chicken house (one of the Carter boys was raising eggs to sell), and then followed a path through an old apple orchard—watching out for yellowjackets along the way—that emerged finally at the edge of the field.

Usually we went directly out to the court, but Mrs. Trask began by showing me through her house that first day. It surprised me by being quite modern and new-looking inside, not like a barn at all. There was a big, high-ceilinged living room with a railed gallery running around it, and bedrooms off the gallery—the old loft, she explained. It was furnished with colorful rugs and wood carvings and brasses and paintings, and a glossy Steinway grand piano Pat would have loved to get her fingers on. The Trasks had lived all over the world, it seemed; Mr. Trask was some kind of engineer, semi-retired now. At the moment he was doing consultant work in New York.

"So we're settled at last," Mrs. Trask said with satisfaction. "Now at least, when the children come home for a visit, they'll know where home *is*."

She took me into the kitchen and offered me a brownie from a batch she'd baked that morning. I didn't really want it, but I took it to be polite. It was hard to imagine Mrs. Trask doing anything so ordinary and domestic as baking brownies, even though she seemed much less formidable here in her own home, chatting casually to me as if I were just another guest. She wore an old shirt and denim pants, in which she somehow looked as elegant and well-groomed as ever, and the dark glasses. I'd thought maybe she wouldn't have to wear them indoors, but evidently she did. I was getting used to them, but even so, it's kind of a weird feeling, never seeing another person's eyes.

While I ate the brownie, Mrs. Trask told me something about her children. There were four of them, all grown. Her married daughter Kate had just had her second baby; she was the one I'd meet later in the summer. There were two sons, one a doctor in the Midwest, the other a geologist currently stationed in South America. Andrea, the youngest, had dropped out of college, lived in a commune for a while, then gone to London to study acting, quit that for a secretarial job, and now had decided to get married.

"For lack of anything better to do, I'm afraid," Mrs. Trask said drily, which I thought was a funny attitude for a mother to take. But before I could ponder this, she looked at her watch and announced it was time we got to work.

Once on the tennis court, Mrs. Trask was all business again. I'd hoped we'd start right in on my serve, but at first our practice sessions were confined to ground strokes. There were various drills. For instance, Mrs. Trask would have me hit nothing but down-the-line forehands for as long as fifteen minutes at a time; then the same thing with the backhand;

105

then nothing but cross-court shots. Sometimes I'd be instructed to hit the ball flat, sometimes to put top-spin on it, sometimes to slice or chop it. Mrs. Trask insisted that I know exactly what I was doing on each shot, and also that I become conscious of my body in a way I never had before.

"You have an exceptionally strong wrist and forearm, Dulcie," she'd tell me. "And that's fine—but because of it you tend to hit your drives with too much arm and not enough body. Your forehand particularly." And she showed me a stance that would help bring the weight of my shoulders and torso around behind the ball.

Or: "You're naturally quick, but your footwork is just plain sloppy a lot of the time. I want to see you start getting into position the minute the ball is hit, instead of depending on a last-minute dash. It's a waste of energy, for one thing—a smart opponent could run you right off the court in a three-set match."

I'd wondered how Mrs. Trask would manage on the court as my practice partner—after all, she'd said herself she didn't really play any more—but she settled that the first day. "You're going to have to hit your shots right to me, Dulcie," she said calmly. "Not just because of my advanced age, but because I have trouble seeing the ball otherwise. Think of me as a kind of human target. It'll be good practice for you. If you're not accurate, you simply don't get the ball back."

It was the only reference she made to her eyesight. She had beautiful, effortless-looking strokes and seemed to be able to place the ball wherever she wanted; but it was true that if she had to take more than a few steps to return a shot of mine, she was apt to mis-hit the ball, or even miss it entirely. This was painful and sad to watch, and I was glad when she didn't even try to move, but just planted herself on the baseline—acting, as she had said, like a human target.

There were times when this bothered me, of course, and I wished for a partner who'd just return the ball no matter what. One day Mrs. Trask had me working on a flat cross-court shot, no topspin allowed, and therefore (it seemed to me) no control possible. I hit forehand after forehand into the net or out into the alley, or else missed getting the angle entirely and sent the ball down the center of the court. Mrs. Trask made no comment, patiently watching each ball sail by, then bending to take another one from the bucket at her feet and send it across to me. Finally we'd used up all the balls and had to stop to collect them.

"I'm sorry!" I said, almost in tears. "I just can't seem to hit it anywhere near you."

But all she said was, "Feet, Dulcie, and shoulders. Where's the net?"

After a moment's thought, I deciphered this as meaning I needed to turn my body further sideways as I hit the ball. I did, and it helped. I was beginning to realize that Mrs. Trask often abbreviated her suggestions deliberately, in order to make me think, instead of just following instructions automatically.

We went on to work on the same flat shot off the backhand, and I did better with that, maybe because you tend to get your body further around for a backhand; even so, I had to fight a natural tendency to hit slightly under the ball.

I must have been concentrating grimly, because finally Mrs. Trask called out with a laugh, "All right, relax, Dulcie. I know it's not easy, and we'll work on it more another day. Just remember, though, your flat strokes are the ones with the real speed, and the more accurately you learn to hit them, the better. Almost anybody can hit the ball cross-court with plenty of spin on it, but that slows it down and makes it easier for your opponent to return it. A good flat cross-court drive . . . well, that's a real weapon."

We had hot sunny weather all that first week. The sun blazed down on the court in the middle of the field, and the old horse cropped away nearby at the dry grass whose smell tickled my nose and sometimes made me sneeze. Mrs. Trask took to wearing a floppy white sun hat that looked absurdly stylish in that setting, and once she asked if I didn't want to borrow a hat for myself. "Doesn't the sun bother you at all, Dulcie? I notice you never wear dark glasses."

"No. I hate the feel of them," I said; and then,

feeling embarrassed—after all, Mrs. Trask apparently had no choice in the matter—I added quickly, "But if you think I ought to wear them. . . ."

"Heavens, no. You're just lucky you can take this sun without even squinting. Do you want to take a break?"

We'd been working on my footwork, with Mrs. Trask hitting the ball from one corner to another, sometimes varying the pace, sometimes hitting short, but insisting that I return to position at the center of the baseline after each shot. I started to go up to the net on one of the short balls, but she waved me back, calling, "Position, Dulcie! And anyway, that wasn't a good approach shot."

Approach shots . . . now that was the kind of thing I wanted to learn. So even though I was a little out of breath and was getting a blister on one foot where I'd worn a hole through the sole of my old frayed sneaker, I shook my head and said I'd just as soon keep going. The sooner we worked our way through all this backcourt drill the better.

As though she guessed what I was thinking, Mrs. Trask smiled and said, "Dulcie, I know it's been said a million times, but it's still true: ground strokes are the foundation of the game. No matter how brilliant you are at the net, or how strongly you serve, you won't last long without a solid backcourt game. And yours can be very good indeed if you work on it. You have a natural sense of timing, you move gracefully

—don't make a face, I'm not complimenting you on your appearance, I'm talking about the way you use your arms and legs, and your racket as an extension of yourself."

She looked at me with that detached professional air I still found a little unnerving. "It's unusual in a player of your physical type, you know—short and compactly built, without a long reach. Most of them stick to the net as much as possible, and when they're forced into the backcourt, they concentrate on retrieving the ball, trading shots until they can maneuver themselves up to the net again. But you . . ." She gave a shrug. "Well, I agree the net's probably going to be your game, Dulcie; but what's wrong with being able to hit a winner from the baseline once in a while?"

This was an unusually long speech for Mrs. Trask, who mostly confined herself to brief comments on whatever I was doing right or wrong. Feeling rather dazed—and secretly a little exhilarated—I walked back to my position on the baseline, prepared to go on fighting the battle of the backcourt.

"Why are you limping?" Mrs. Trask said sharply, in her old, abrupt way.

"My sneaker—it's got a hole in it."

"Well, for heaven's sake, child, go out and buy a new pair! If there's one thing a tennis player learns to take care of, it's her feet."

By the time I got home each afternoon—walking from the recreation center, as I insisted I preferred to

do—I did feel pretty footsore, and my muscles ached. I'd try to relax for a while with a book or some music, but after only a few minutes in the empty house I'd begin to feel restless. Soon I'd be on my feet again, aimlessly sweeping the kitchen floor or cleaning out a cupboard that didn't really need it—anything to keep from thinking about my family. Because of course I hadn't told them yet.

It's funny, but as long as I was on the tennis court, nothing existed but the bounce of the ball, the thud of my racket, the feel of my own moving body, all enclosed in the silence of field and sky. I literally didn't think about anything but tennis, nor did we talk of anything else. Which I supposed was the way Mrs. Trask wanted it: a separate world, apart from anything that had gone before.

But at home: "Dulcie, you look kind of tired these days. What's the matter, the job getting to be too much for you?"

Or: "Dulcie, I asked you to change the sheets today! It's not like you to forget. Maybe you'd better start coming home from the center a little earlier. I know you have fun fooling around with your friends over there, and that's all right, but it shouldn't be at the expense of your other responsibilities. After all, with Pat taking Eric off your hands . . ."

Eric said, "Look how tan Dulcie's getting."

"All that sunbathing," my father teased. "Lying around the pool looking glamorous all day. Who's the boyfriend this week, Boots?"

For some reason this last remark made me see red. "Daddy, I have boys as friends, I do *not* have boyfriends. I'm only thirteen, for Pete's sake!"

"Yes, Norman, don't rush her," my mother said, sounding amused. "Six months from now, maybe a year—just let nature take its course."

At which Pat made a rude noise and turned away. Later, as we were washing up the supper dishes together, she said, "I'm sorry, but that kind of talk makes me *sick*. You better watch it, Dulcie, they've got your life all figured out for you. Let's see, you can be on all the dance committees at school, and maybe you can run for class secretary; but not president, of course, that's a job for a boy, or some pushy-type girl. In high school you'll get to be a cheerleader, what else? As for college—well, maybe you can go to one of those big universities out west where they still have things like Homecoming Queens. You know, riding on a float, wearing a long dress, and waving and smiling like some big doll, just another part of the mechanism." She rubbed savagely at the glass she was drying. "At least that's a fate I'll be spared."

"Oh, come on, Pat." It always upset me when she talked that way—I don't think she realized how much. "Mom and Dad aren't that bad. And anyway, I'll have something to say about my own future, won't I?"

She gave me a look. "Will you? Well, let's hope so. Hey, by the way," she said, changing the subject, though not as much as she thought, "I heard you played a set of tennis the other day against Mark Leonard, of all people, and almost beat him!"

"Well, not quite," I said uncomfortably. The good old grapevine. "He was pretty wild."

"Yes, he's apt to be. But still, what on earth possessed you?" Pat asked curiously.

"Oh . . . I was just looking for a game, and so was he."

Evidently Mark hadn't said anything about Mrs. Trask. Maybe he'd been hoping she'd offer to coach him; or maybe he still had no idea who she was. Not that I really did either, I reminded myself. I'd kept waiting for her to make some reference to her own tennis career, but so far she hadn't, and I felt shy about asking her. For all I knew, she'd been just a good club player in her day, nothing more. What really mattered was the fact that she was a good teacher. Still, I couldn't help feeling curious.

Pat finished drying the last glass and hung up her dish towel. "I'm going to the movies with Laura. You want to come?"

"No, thanks," I said. I was tired and wanted to get to bed early. Also I'd just remembered the big tennis encyclopedia Pat kept up in our room. It had been a Christmas present from our parents—one of those oversized volumes full of glossy photographs and not much text; but it covered all the major tennis players of modern times, meaning the last forty or fifty years.

As soon as Pat had left the house, I went upstairs and pulled the heavy book out of the bookcase —a coffee-table book, Pat had said ungratefully; who cares what all those old characters looked like, anyway? But at the moment I did. I began leafing through the slick, shiny pages, studying the pictures of the women players. Helen Wills, Helen Jacobs, Alice Marble, a lot of other people I'd never heard of . . . no, that was too far back, anyway. I flipped over a few more pages. Sarah Palfrey Cooke, Pauline Betz. Well, I knew she wasn't anyone as famous as that, and as for all of these other women in their old-fashioned tennis dresses, wearing dark lipstick and funny hairdos—well, without even a first name to go by. . . .

I'd been turning pages rapidly; now I turned back to a picture that had caught my eye in passing. The angle of the head, the square shape of the shoulders. . . . Could it be? I studied the photograph carefully: a slender, dark-haired girl in a pleated tennis dress, slightly crouched in the ready position, her racket in front of her, supported by her right hand but held in her left. She was smiling slightly, but her eyes were intent, her whole body concentrated and alert.

The caption under the photograph read:

ANN LOEFFLER. One of the outstanding young players of the pre-war period, until her early retirement in 1942. Noted for her strong serve and tireless backcourt game. At the net, her backhand volley was considered one of the finest in women's tennis.

There followed a list of titles, mostly European ones that didn't mean much to me, and a record of performance in major tournaments. I noted that she had twice made the quarter-finals at Wimbledon, and had been a semi-finalist at Forest Hills.

Wimbledon and Forest Hills! The girl in the photograph didn't look more than seventeen or eighteen. How old could she have been when she retired? And how far might she have gone if she'd kept on playing? I examined the picture again, the confident smiling girl. No, I wasn't mistaken: this was my Mrs. Trask thirty years ago, at the beginning of a career that had ended too soon, for whatever reason.

I put the book away and went into the bathroom to brush my teeth. All right, Dulcie, I told the face in the mirror. You've got to tell Mom and Dad. How long do you think you can keep it a secret, anyway? (But I thought of the Carters' tennis court in the middle of the field—in the middle of nowhere, really, so far as anyone else was concerned; and how Mrs. Trask was a newcomer to town, and unlikely to know anyone my parents knew.) You're going to go to them and say you've met a tennis coach, she used to be a top player herself—look, here's her picture in Pat's book—and listen, Mom and Dad, she thinks I have talent, she's willing to coach me for free, she'd like me to put in three hours' practice a day if possible. . . .

Sure. And they'll say, What about Pat? Has she seen Pat play?

They'll say: But Dulcie, you've never shown that much interest in tennis before, you can't possibly be serious about this thing! If you really want to play that much, you can always go over to the club; maybe we can even arrange for a few lessons with Jack if you'd like. But three hours a day, just practicing—why, that's fantastic! We'd better talk to this woman, whoever she is, make her understand that aside from anything else, you're just not the type. A passing phase, a fad—lots of girls go through them at your age, and of course tennis is the In Thing this year. But after all, you're only thirteen!

They'll say: Why didn't you tell us about this right away? Really, Dulcie, to go behind our backs like this, sneaking off without letting anybody know where you were going. . . .

But still, I thought unhappily, as I got into bed, I've got to tell them.

Mrs. Trask said the same thing next day, after our session on the court. As we were making our way back through the grape arbor, she said, "Oh, Dulcie, I meant to ask you—what about the weekend?"

"The weekend?" I ducked under a swinging tendril of vine.

"Well, today's Friday. I know you'll want to spend time with your family, but I thought if you could spare an hour or two on Sunday. . . . I'd like to start working on service returns," she explained, "but my own serve doesn't amount to much any more, and I thought either my husband or Johnny Carter. . . . Dulcie?"

She turned to look at me as we emerged onto the broad expanse of the driveway that glittered with mica chips in the sunlight. "What's the matter?"

"Well, I just don't know about the weekend, Mrs. Trask. I mean . . ."

"I see. You haven't spoken to your parents yet. Is that it?"

"No." I shifted my racket under my arm. "But you said . . . we both said we'd wait and see how things went, and it's only been a week—"

"A week is long enough, Dulcie. I simply cannot go on working with you without your parents' knowledge and permission. You do realize that, don't you?" I nodded. "That's assuming *you* want to go on, of course."

"Oh, I do! I mean—I've learned so much already, just in one week."

"Not as much as you think," Mrs. Trask said with a smile. "But you've worked hard, Dulcie, and I'm satisfied that you have the basic equipment for the game, and the temperament—on the court, at any rate." She studied me for a moment, and then walked briskly over to where the Mercedes stood parked beside her neat border of pink-and-white petunias. "When you talk to your parents, though, I want you to make it clear that I'm not guaranteeing anything. You have promise. That's about all anyone can say at this point."

When I was silent, she said in a gentler tone, "I assume they're not ogres, are they—these parents of yours?"

"Oh, no. It's just—well, I'll talk to them this weekend, Mrs. Trask, really I will."

But I didn't say much on the ride back to town. I'd meant to tell Mrs. Trask about the picture I'd found—there were a hundred questions I wanted to ask her—but somehow I wasn't in the mood any more. As she let me off at the recreation center, she said, "Then I'll expect you on Sunday, shall I?"

"I— Maybe I'd better call and let you know."

"All right. And Dulcie, new sneakers, yes?"

"Yes."

I smiled; but my steps lagged on the way home, and not just because of my sore feet.

eight

I PROMISED myself I'd get it over with right away, that same evening. But I'd forgotten Dad would be working late—on Fridays the store stays open until nine—and by the time he got home, Mom had gone to bed with a headache. A rough week, she said, with Dr. Hebert covering for another dentist who was on vacation and whose patients had to be fitted in somehow.

She did look worn out, showing her age for once, as she went upstairs with a magazine and a glass of Ovaltine. (To Pat's disgust, she won't take vitamins; but she swears by Ovaltine.) I couldn't help wondering if there were ever times when she really enjoyed her work—when it *gave* her something, instead of just draining her. I knew she'd gotten her training originally for what she called practical reasons: as long as people have teeth, they'll need dentists, and dentists will always need nurses.

Security, a dependable income— I'm sure Mom's good at her work, efficient and quick, but what does it really mean to her? A friend of Pat's said once, when we were discussing women's lib, "Well, look at your mother—I mean, *she's* liberated, she goes out to work," and we both just laughed and shook our heads, a little sadly.

Saturday morning Eric was invited to a birthday party down the street. I'd been asked to help out, so I went along too. You'd think I would have been sick of little kids by then, after a couple of weeks at the Morrisons', but the fact is I love birthday parties, and I get a kick out of Eric and his pals when they're all dressed up (well, clean, anyway) and sort of nervous and excited. So for a couple of hours I blew up balloons and helped organize a three-legged race and a peanut hunt and a penny-pitching contest and made sure everyone got a prize for something-or-other, until it was time to herd them all inside for milk and sandwiches and birthday cake. Two of the little boys began throwing peppermints at each other, but I broke that up and sent them all outside again, where they ran around in their birthday hats whooping and wrestling and blowing noisemakers at each other, and generally having their usual grubby good time now that the special part of the party was over.

"You're so good with them, Dulcie," the mother said tiredly, as we cleaned up the shambles in the dining room. "They always seem to *listen* to you. Here, you take the rest of the cake home with you, and thanks a million."

By the time I got back with Eric, everyone else had finished lunch, and the plan was to spend the afternoon at the club—where else? But I hadn't been over there in quite a while, and the thought of a swim appealed to me after my hot and sticky morning. Pat said something about our playing some doubles later on, if I felt like it. I figured she'd probably wind up playing with her own friends as usual, and anyway, I didn't mind the thought of a day off from tennis; but with Mom telling me to hurry up, I ran to collect my racket and sneakers . . .

Sneakers. "Dad," I said, as we all piled into the old station wagon, "could we stop at Sandler's on the way, just for a minute?"

"Well, it's not exactly *on* the way, sweetheart. What do you need?"

"Just some new sneakers. Please, it won't take long, I know my size and everything."

"Oh, Dulcie." My mother sighed. "It's Saturday, and they'll probably be crowded. Can't you wait till next week?"

I held up my old sneakers to show her.

"Good heavens! What have you been doing,

jumping around on hot coals? All right," she said resignedly. "Sandler's it is, and let's hope it won't take more than twenty minutes."

It didn't take long, and I bought some peds to go with them—the silly kind with a pompon at the heel, which was all they had—so I wouldn't get more blisters from playing in brand-new tennis shoes. Dad gave me the money for them, and that made me feel a little guilty. After all, he didn't really know why I needed them. Tonight I'll talk to them, I told myself. Tonight for sure.

The club was crowded, with lots of people waiting for courts. I swam for a while and talked to some of the kids, who wanted to know where I'd been lately, and even let Barry Fox buy me an ice cream bar. After all, I hadn't had any lunch except for half a sandwich at the birthday party, and even though Barry thinks he's just too much—he plays the trumpet and has a pool table in his basement—he can be quite funny when he gets clowning around. Also I was feeling sort of lazy and relaxed for a change. No tennis today, I thought, not with this mob and the weekend rule that gives adults precedence over kids on the courts. I realized I'd been feeling a little nervous about the prospect of playing with Pat, I wasn't exactly sure why.

And then Pat appeared, looking for me among the crowd of swimmers to say there'd be a court free in ten minutes or so, and the Whittaker twins wanted

123

to play, and how about it? I could feel the other kids eyeing her curiously as we stood talking—Pat looking very tall and brown in a tunic-type tennis dress with her dark hair held in place by a broad white headband. She hardly ever came over to the pool area, saying she didn't care about swimming; but I knew it was partly because she felt self-conscious in a bathing suit—which didn't make any sense to me. Pat really has a terrific figure, and if she were wearing a bikini, no one would even notice her face. Not that they do anyway, not nearly as much as she thinks. But also, I guess, she thinks of the tennis courts as her territory, a place where people know and respect her, and she feels safe. Maybe she even feels invisible there, in a way, wearing the same uniform as everyone else.

I had no such uniform as usual, just the striped shirt and cut-off jeans I'd worn to the birthday party. There was a chocolate icing smudge on the front of the shirt, which I tried to rub out with water from the bathhouse tap, but all it did was smear. Pat looked at me critically as we walked across the grass toward the courts.

"It's a good thing they don't enforce the rule about wearing whites on the weekend," she said. "Honestly, Dulcie . . ."

"I didn't have time to change before we left," I said defensively.

"Well, can't you at least do something about your hair? It's soaking wet."

"Sorry!" I said, getting mad. "I certainly don't want to embarrass you in front of your friends."

"Oh, the twins . . ." Pat shrugged. "They don't matter. In fact we should beat them easily. No, it's just the principle of the thing."

What principle? Sometimes Pat is a lot like Mom.

I don't know exactly what I thought was going to happen on the court—that I'd amaze everyone with my new championship style, my blazing baseline drives, my lightning footwork? That Pat would say, "Dulcie, what's happened to your tennis, it's absolutely spectacular!" and urge me to enter the next tournament in her place?

In fact I played terrible, sloppy tennis, and we were lucky to win at all. My serve was the same old nothing, of course, and as for my ground strokes—well, after hitting a fairly hard ball all week, I just couldn't seem to adjust to the gentle, loopy stuff the twins kept sending over. My timing was completely off. I'd get into position quickly, as Mrs. Trask had taught me, and then wait for what seemed like whole minutes at a time to begin my swing, with the result that I lost all rhythm and momentum. If I tried to hit the ball hard, I usually sent it into the net; if I tried to loop it back softly, playing their game, it would go sailing out. Maybe that sounds contradictory, but anyone who's ever played pat-ball will know exactly what I mean.

Pat stayed in the backcourt, playing her steady

game, her accuracy making up for my errors. I urged her to come up to the net on her serve, but she shook her head, saying the twins would just lob over our heads.

"But look at the way they're playing," I argued. "One up and one back half the time. All we have to do is get up there and knock the ball down the middle, in between them."

"Oh, listen, Dulcie, don't sweat it. Just keep getting the ball back"—she gave me a look that said clearly, *if you can*—"and we can't lose."

Which is the kind of tennis I hate—long, pointless rallies where nobody even tries to place the ball, you just wait until somebody hits a weaker shot than usual. I couldn't get to the net on my dinky serve, and although I positioned myself there on Pat's serve, there was nothing to do but drop back after the return, since she wouldn't come up. I was darned if *we'd* play one up and one back, even though we might have won some points that way, the twins being out of position most of the time.

We played two sets, winning them 6–4 and 6–3, if you can call it winning. During the last few games our parents strolled up with some friends to watch. As we walked off the court, Dad said, "Well, well, sisters against sisters. A real blood match."

One of the twins—Marcy, I think, I can never tell them apart—grinned and said, "Oh, no, that's when you play your own sister," and everyone laughed.

Dad patted me on the shoulder. "Well, Boots, you work on those ground strokes of yours, and who knows? . . . Maybe someday you'll be giving Pat a run for her money."

I was speechless with rage and humiliation; but even if I could have spoken, this was hardly the time to announce that I'd been selected for coaching by a real tennis teacher, and that it was partly *because* of my ground strokes. I wouldn't have blamed him for thinking I'd flipped completely. Later, I told myself, later. But it was going to be harder than ever now, I realized wretchedly; in fact it was probably going to sound just plain nutty.

"Ladies' doubles," Mrs. Trask said with a sigh, when I told her about this one day. "It can be the best game in the world, or the worst. When I think of all those women getting a little polite exercise and calling it tennis. . . . But still, Dulcie," she told me sternly, "a good tennis player is like a good pianist —he can get music out of the most beat-up old piano, and never mind how out of tune it is or how many of the keys stick. It's a matter of concentration and technique, and giving your best no matter what the circumstances. A real pro learns to adjust to almost anything."

I thought about that and realized that whenever you're feeling a little superior and critical, impatient to play your own game and not your opponent's, your concentration is the first thing to go. As for technique, well, if you're not really even seeing the ball, you're certainly not going to hit it properly. And then, because you're playing badly against an opponent you didn't respect in the first place, you get upset, and it's almost impossible to get your concentration back. A kind of vicious circle.

By the time we got home late that afternoon, I'd decided to wait until my parents were having their Saturday night drink before dinner in the family room. They'd be relaxed then and ready to listen, and I would explain the whole thing calmly, not making excuses for my poor showing that day—I didn't want to seem to be putting Pat down, that was the last thing I wanted—and if they didn't believe me (which was all too likely), why we'd call up Mrs. Trask and they could talk to her, and she'd convince them.

I just hoped Pat wouldn't be around. And that was funny, because I knew that in a way Pat was the one person who would really understand; but I wasn't sure what this would do to the good kind of feelings we'd always had about each other, in spite of everything. . . . We'd never been rivals before, and I was afraid that was how she'd think of my new interest in tennis—as a challenge to her. It had nothing to do with her, but could I make her understand that?

As it turned out, though, nobody was around that evening except Eric. Pat was going to an outdoor concert in Stamford with some friends, my parents had a dinner party invitation, and I was the baby-sitter. No one had bothered to tell me any of this beforehand, and although normally I wouldn't have thought anything about it, tonight I felt resentful and put-upon.

What if I'd had a date? I thought. In fact, Barry Fox had asked me to go to some party with him tonight. I'd told him my parents didn't allow me to date yet—not true, of course; the only rule I would have been breaking was my mother's about never accepting a last-minute invitation ("it cheapens you")— but the fact was I just didn't want to go. A bunch of kids fooling around, experimenting with smoking and drinking and maybe pot as well. . . . The last few parties I'd gone to had been like that, and I just couldn't see the point.

Still, I felt grumpy and cross. After everyone had left—my mother in a swish of long skirts and perfume, seemingly quite restored from her bad week —I heated up some frozen pizza for Eric and me, and we sat eating it in silence until Eric began on his favorite subject: dogs.

"Oh, Eric!" I snapped. "When are you ever going to learn that you just can't have everything you want!"

He looked hurt, but said earnestly, "This isn't everything, it's just one important thing. My important *big* thing is getting a dog."

"I know, but . . ."

I stopped. I knew just how he felt. Wait a year, everybody had told him, including me; but I thought now, if Eric wants a dog that much, I bet he really would do most of the work himself. He's not too young if he cares enough. His school is nearby, so he could come home at lunchtime and take the dog for a run. As for building a pen—because Mom wouldn't want the dog in the house any more than necessary, that was for sure—well, Eric's pretty good with his hands. If Dad knocked in a few posts for him, and we got some wire. . . .

But I didn't say anything; instead I changed the subject to dessert, which almost always works. I said I'd be the soda jerk and Eric could be the customer and order anything he wanted—which turned out to be a wild concoction of graham crackers, peanut butter, three kinds of ice cream, marshmallows, whipped cream, and maple syrup. Eric wanted raisins on top, but I drew the line at that. Then we watched TV until Eric's bedtime, and after he'd brushed his teeth and gotten into pajamas, I let him read me a story. This involved a lot of long pauses and loud breathing while he puzzled over the hard words, but he wouldn't let me help him; he's very proud of his reading.

He went to sleep almost immediately, which he hardly ever does when Mom and Dad are home. Usually he comes downstairs two or three times during the evening, or pretends to be scared of the dark, or needs another drink of water; and even though they'll say, "Oh, Eric, not *again!*" they never really scold him. They were always very strict about bedtime with Pat and me when we were little. It's one of the things that bugs Pat about our parents.

Maybe it was that crazy dessert, but although I stayed up fairly late watching the *Saturday Night Movie,* I couldn't get to sleep for a long time. I heard Pat come in, humming softly under her breath and moving quietly around the room so as not to disturb me; but when she stopped once and whispered, "Dulcie? Are you awake?" I lay still and didn't answer.

I thought: Maybe it will rain tomorrow.

But Sunday morning was cloudless, sunny and cool, the best day we'd had in a week of good weather. My parents slept late, and then, over sausages and French toast—I'd cooked a good breakfast, trying to put my best foot forward, or something—said they thought they'd go to church and did anyone else want to come? They're usually pretty casual about church in the summertime, but the visiting minister today was the brother of an old friend of Mom's, and they thought they should put in an appearance.

"In good tennis weather too," Dad said. "That really ought to impress him. In fact I'm impressed with myself. Are there any more sausages, Boots?"

My mother wanted to know whether her pink suit had come back from the cleaners and, by the way, wasn't that a weird outfit Shirley Edmonds had on last night, and really some people should act their age. My father said he hadn't noticed, and Mom said, like fun you didn't, and they began hashing over the party while they drank their coffee.

I was starting to feel frantic. I knew they wouldn't be home from church until noon at least, maybe later if they stayed to chat with the minister afterwards—and I ought to call Mrs. Trask this morning, in fact, I should have called her before.

"Heavens, look at the time!" My mother pushed back her chair. "I've got to get dressed. And Norman, what do you want to do about the Parkers? I promised Betty I'd let her know this morning."

"About going down to the beach, you mean? Well, I don't know, I was looking forward to some tennis this afternoon—but let's see what the kids want to do. Eric," he called out the screen door into the yard, where Eric was flying his remote-control helicopter, "you want to go to the beach today?"

"Mom!" I said, more loudly than I'd intended, as she stood up from the table. "Dad! Please. I've got to talk to you."

They both looked at me.

"Well?" Dad said, as I hesitated. "What is it, Boots?"

"Better make it quick, whatever it is," Mom said, glancing at the clock again. "And what about the beach, Dulcie, do you want to go? Because if you don't . . ."

"Well, that's one of the things I need to ask you about," I said desperately. "I mean, I sort of had a tennis date this afternoon, only—only I said I'd talk to you first and explain, because . . ."

"Can I take my inner tube?" Eric demanded from the doorway.

"Wait a minute, Eric," Dad said, pouring himself another cup of coffee. "A tennis date, Boots? Well, fine, if you don't mind missing the beach. Who with?"

"Well, that's the thing," I began, and at the same moment Eric said, "Tommy Howard has a raft, can Tommy come with us? Will there be a lot of those rocks that hurt your feet?"

"That depends on the tide," my mother told him. "And it's just our family that's invited, Eric. Now calm down, we're trying to listen to Dulcie."

They were both looking at me again, waiting patiently. I took a deep breath and said, "Her name is Mrs. Trask."

They looked blank. "Mrs. Trask?" Dad said. "Do we know her?"

"No, she's just moved here. They live out on Wagon Hill Road, next door to some people named Carter, and they have a tennis court—the Carters do, I mean . . ."

"Oh, yes, the old farm," Mom said, looking interested. "Mrs. Carter's a patient of Dr. Hebert's. Loads of money," she told my father, "but you'd never know it from the way she dresses. . . . You've seen her around, Norman. She's on the school board, and last year she headed up the United Fund or one of those charity things."

Dad said, "I wonder where they buy their hardware."

"I'm not *talking* about the Carters!" I almost shouted. "I'm talking about Mrs. Trask! She knows a lot about tennis, in fact she used to be a really good player herself, and she's interested in me, she wants to help me—coaching me, you know, working on my strokes—only she said I had to make sure it was okay with you."

I stopped for breath, knowing I ought to tell them now about the past week, and Dad said, "Hey, take it easy, Boots! Well, sure it's okay, why not? I mean, if this Mrs. Trask can spare the time, and it's what you want to do. . . ." He shrugged.

"But it's a *lot* of time!" I said wildly. I had the feeling they were listening to me without really hearing me. "A couple of hours a day, at least. Oh, don't worry," I went on hastily, seeing Mom's expression change, "I can do it after my job at the Morrisons' and still get my work done here, but . . . well, I might have to go over there on weekends too sometimes, like today."

"Yes, what about that?" My mother frowned distractedly. "I mean, how are you going to get there, Dulcie? Because if we have to take you clear out to Wagon Hill Road before we even start for the beach—"

"Oh, Mrs. Trask will pick me up and bring me home."

"Well, fine, no problem." Dad stretched, and threw a mock punch in Eric's direction. "You coming to church with us, old man?" he said and laughed when Eric made a face. "Sounds like a good deal, Boots. Private court, transportation. . . . Hey, Eric, you think you still remember how to swim in salt water?"

Mom had opened the door of the freezer and was muttering to herself. "Chicken tonight. I guess, we can cook it outside. Dulcie, be an angel and make us some sandwiches to take to the beach, will you? And let's see, lemonade and fruit and the rest of the cake. We had a late breakfast, we ought to be able to survive till then. What are the Carters like?" she asked over her shoulder.

"Johnny Carter?" Pat said, coming into the kitchen in her old bathrobe with her hair wound up in a towel. "*Those* Carters?"

I said, "The only one I've met is the youngest boy. His name is Stuart, he's about nine, and he raises chickens." My voice was shaking, but nobody seemed to notice. "Anyway, the Carters aren't the point. The point is—"

"What about Johnny Carter?" my mother asked Pat.

"Oh . . ." Pat shrugged elaborately. "He graduated year before last. Sort of tall and quite brainy. I think he goes to Princeton, one of those big deal places."

Mom nodded, as if everything about Johnny Carter had been explained. "Well," she said briskly, "I'm never going to make it to church if I don't get a move on."

"Darn, I wish you'd told me you were going. I just washed my hair."

"You can use my drier if you want. Oh, there goes the phone, it's probably Betty Parker. Answer it, will you, Pat, and I'll take it upstairs." She rushed out of the kitchen, her slippers clacking on the tiles.

I turned to my father, who was having a wresling match with Eric. "Dad," I said urgently. "I'm really serious about this. About tennis, I mean, and working hard. The thing is—well—maybe I could be really *good* someday."

"I'm sure you could, Boots. Maybe this—what's her name again?—this Mrs. Trask can straighten out that serve of yours; that would certainly help. *Watch it, Eric, the orange juice!*" He reached out to steady the table while Eric pummeled him from behind. "Who didn't finish their juice, anyway? We can't afford to waste food around here, not with prices the way they are these days."

I turned away then and began clearing the table, plunging the dishes into the hot, soapy water, setting the sausage pan aside to soak, unplugging the coffee pot. My eyes stung as if I might be going to sneeze; but if I'd made a sound right then, I don't know whether it would have come out as a sob or a laugh.

Maybe I should have told them about Ann Loeffler, I thought. Maybe the name would have meant something to them. But I wasn't a hundred percent sure, just from the picture, and anyway . . . anyway, I told myself, it's better this way. After all, you were the one who didn't want to make a big deal out of the whole thing. Now you can just concentrate on tennis, you won't be going behind anybody's back, and there won't be any pressure at home. I didn't even feel a qualm about my deception; obviously my parents didn't care when I started, last week or next week or never. Really, when I thought about it, things couldn't have worked out better.

So when I called Mrs. Trask later that morning, I was able to tell her with perfect truth that I'd talked to my parents, and that everything was absolutely okay with them.

nine

BY THE MIDDLE of August, my new sneakers were stained green with court dust, and I'd gone through three pairs of peds. We'd begun work on my serve, but I was still doing a lot of running. In fact, some of the time, running was all I did, most of it backwards. Mrs. Trask said if I was going to make the most of my net game, I had to be able to move quickly and easily in any direction, and that backwards was hardest for most people. So forward and back I'd run, charging the net, then backpedaling as fast as I could to the baseline; or sometimes dodging from side to side, then moving back on a diagonal or turning to chase an imaginary lob. All this with a racket in my hand but no ball in play, which sometimes made me feel pretty stupid.

138

On rainy days when we couldn't have practice, Mrs. Trask urged me to go out and jog. Well, that wasn't too bad. Some of the kids I knew were trying out for the girls' track team, and you'd see them out running from time to time; so I didn't feel too conspicuous as I splashed along the roads near home. But when it came to doing things like push-ups—to strengthen my arms and shoulders—I made sure I was alone, where no one would walk in on me. I could just imagine what my family would have to say about that.

Ball tossing was another kind of indoor practice, something Mrs. Trask wanted me to do whenever I could. "Your serve absolutely depends on a consistent toss," she told me. "You ought to be able to place the ball exactly the same way each time. And I mean *exactly*—to within a fraction of an inch, and always at the same pace. So you can't practice your toss enough, Dulcie, and you don't need any equipment for that except a ball. Do it over and over again, a hundred times, a thousand, until it becomes absolutely automatic.

Pat caught me at this one evening in our room. I was standing between our two beds, concentrating so hard on the lift of my arm and the release of the ball ("Smoothly, Dulcie, no wrist motion—just let it go") that I didn't even hear her open the door.

"You're lucky you're short," she remarked, watching me. "The ceiling's too low for me. Also it's such a boring thing to practice. How's it going, anyway? Your strokes must be improving a lot, with all the time you're putting in."

I hadn't said much about my tennis at home, and I'd avoided any more weekend confrontations at the club. My parents treated the subject casually, when they thought of it at all. As far as Pat knew, my so-called coaching sessions amounted to nothing more than a few sets of singles with some eccentric older woman who wanted a regular opponent and was willing to give me a few pointers in exchange. Certainly Pat herself had never done the kind of concentrated drilling Mrs. Trask was putting me through.

Often I was tempted to tell her about it, especially now that my serve was beginning to take shape. Hey, listen, Pat, I wanted to say, I'm learning to hit a flat serve, and it's really working for me—nothing fancy, I just hit it as hard and deep as I can; but I can move forward on it, in fact I'm already rushing the net as I follow through (if I don't foot-fault first, something I have to watch), and I'm enjoying it, for the first time I actually *like* serving. It's such a neat feeling when you get your whole body behind the ball, your whole self in a way, all your energy and determination and caring. . . .

But of course all I said now was, "Oh, fine. It's a lot of fun."

Pat said, "Well, sometimes. Of course, playing under pressure is different." She had several tournaments coming up in the next few weeks, and I knew she was beginning to get tense about them.

But I *like* pressure, I wanted to say; that just makes the game more fun . . . only of course I didn't really know that about myself, I thought. I'd never even played in a real tournament.

Pat wandered over to the bookcase and began looking through a pile of records. She said in an off-hand tone, "What's Johnny Carter like? As a player, I mean."

"Well, he's only around on weekends—he has a summer job—so I haven't seen much of him. But he'd be quite good if he played more."

"Nothing like having your own court," Pat said, with what was meant to be a sneer. I knew she was really covering up her curiosity, and had to hide a smile when she put on a Chopin piano record, something she only does when she's in a dreamy kind of mood. Mostly Pat likes modern music, all those electronic screeches and moans and gargling noises.

I said, "Johnny's really nice, though. I mean, he's interested in a lot of things, and he doesn't treat you like a little kid. Me, I mean. He remembered you from school," I added. "He asked how you were, and if you still played the piano."

"Oh, big deal," Pat said; but she kept her face turned away from me, and I could tell she was pleased. I wondered suddenly if I could arrange for Pat to come along with me to the Carters' some weekend. We could play mixed doubles with Johnny and

Mr. Trask, and then maybe Pat and Johnny. . . . But no, I thought. That could really foul things up, having Pat see me there. I wasn't ready for that yet, I wanted things to go along just as they were. . . .

But I did like Johnny, as I'd told Pat, and I thought they might have a lot in common. Maybe Pat would even relax with him. Because Johnny's not the kind who cares anything about appearances—you have the feeling he just looks right through them to whatever's important underneath. His car is typical of him, a battered old Pontiac with a rebuilt engine under the hood. He spends a lot of time tinkering with it, but I don't think he's ever even noticed the ugly dents and patches of rust. As long as it runs, it's beautiful.

Which is sort of the way the whole Carter family seems to operate. Mrs. Trask told me they'd had all the wiring in the old farmhouse redone last year, and put in new steel beams to replace old ones that had sagged badly; but it would never occur to them to have the outside painted, for instance, until the paint was literally falling off the clapboards.

Johnny himself is tall and loosely built, with a long bony face and very sharp blue eyes. He's not really good-looking, except when he smiles—but that smile must have been what Pat remembered about him. I know it put me at ease that first Sunday we played, when I was scared—not so much of Johnny, but of letting Mrs. Trask down. I didn't know what she'd told the Carters about me, but of course they knew about the private coaching, and I thought they might be expecting some kind of child genius. I even wore my tennis dress, to bolster my confidence. Naturally Johnny showed up in old clothes, and his sneakers were in even worse shape than my old ones.

"Service returns, right?" he said, looking down at me with that smile. "I better warn you, Dulcie— my instructions are to blast the ball right by you if I can. Right, Mrs. T? Sounds pretty brutal to me."

"Oh, Dulcie's stronger than she looks," Mrs. Trask told him. "Just serve hard, Johnny, the way you normally would."

"Hard and into the net, usually. Well, fine, I can use the practice."

Still, I could feel he was holding back at first. When he was satisfied that I could actually get the ball back, he increased the pace of his serve and added some spin, so that the ball kicked up and away from me—but to my left, my forehand side.

"Hey," he called to Mrs. Trask in an injured tone. "You didn't tell me she was a lefty."

Mrs. Trask just smiled. After a few more serves, she told Johnny to rush the net so that I could practice trying to pass him; or, on a really hard serve, at least block the ball back at his feet to give him a difficult volley.

"Who's supposed to be getting the workout," Johnny protested, "Dulcie or me?"

It was fun, and sometimes we were tempted to continue the rally beyond the first few shots; but Mrs. Trask intervened firmly. She had me concentrate on position and preparation, the placing of my feet, the angle of my shoulders, the length of my backswing. When I made an error or missed the ball entirely, she made me analyze what I'd done wrong—sometimes over Johnny's complaints that he'd served an honest-to-God ace.

"She wasn't *supposed* to get that one back," he'd say. "That was my bomb!"

"Ah, but she's going to get the bombs back," Mrs. Trask told him. "Dulcie's going to return them all—all but the very best."

"Dulcie," Johnny said solemnly, "I'm sure this isn't good for your ego. Or mine. I mean, do you get the feeling someone's putting me down?"

Playing with Mr. Trask was quite different, and not just because he was older and didn't hit the ball as hard as Johnny. What he lacked in power, he made up in control and touch, varying the amount of spin he put on his serve, sometimes slicing it, sometimes hitting it flat, so that I never knew what to expect. Also he could place the ball much more accurately than Johnny, serving to my weaknesses. But he balked at rushing the net.

"Not unless you two want to carry me back to the house," he told his wife. "I haven't rushed the net in years, and I'm not starting now, not even for a pretty girl." He winked at me.

"I'm sure Laurie would lend you the horse," Mrs. Trask said in the bantering tone they always seemed to use with each other.

Laurie, the Carters' eleven-year-old daughter, was riding the brown mare around in the field. She urged old Sally into a canter as I watched, her hair flying out behind her. I thought how free she looked, and I couldn't help feeling a momentary impatience with Mrs. Trask's discipline. So much starting and stopping and never being able to lose myself in the rhythm of play, which was my own kind of freedom. But of course when it came to service returns, as Mrs. Trask had pointed out, that was the whole psychological problem: you had to be able to hit a good shot from a virtual standstill.

"Oh, sure," Mr. Trask was grumbling. "Horseback riding, that's all I need. Who do you think I am, anyway? John Wayne? Pancho Gonzales?"

Actually I thought Mr. Trask was in pretty good shape for a man his age, though maybe a bit overweight. He had a big solid frame and moved lightly on his feet, as some big men do. His face was square and ruddy, and he had a hearty, booming laugh; but his eyes were shrewd and rather cold. You had the feeling he was used to having things go his way, and that his way would usually be the right one; if other people had to be brushed aside or stepped over, well that was just too bad.

I didn't dislike him; in fact he was very cordial

and pleasant to me, asking me all kinds of questions about home and school and my tastes and interests and opinions on all sorts of things—so that in the course of an hour, he'd learned more about me, in a way, than Mrs. Trask had in several weeks. He was a willing practice partner and generous in his praise of me on the court, often more so than I deserved. Yet I sensed that he didn't really take me very seriously. I was a kind of hobby for his wife, something to occupy her time.

One thing I did learn from Mr. Trask—his wife's first name was Ann. Ann Loeffler, I was sure of that now, the promising young player who had quit tennis for reasons unknown, at least to me. I thought it was odd that neither of them ever referred to her career. When they talked about the past, it was always of places they'd lived, things the children had done, a bridge or a dam Mr. Trask had built in some remote corner of the world. I realized I'd just have to wait until Mrs. Trask herself brought up the subject—if she ever did.

The only person who seemed to share my curiosity was Mrs. Morrison, who sometimes exchanged a few words with Mrs. Trask when she came to pick me up. There was no longer any reason for us to meet furtively over at the recreation center, and having Mrs. Trask drive me door-to-door gave us that much more time on the tennis court. Once Pat was home before me, pinning up Eric's wet suit and towel on the line by the side of the house, but she just waved as we drove up and didn't come out to the car. I hoped Mrs. Trask wouldn't think she was being rude —Pat's shy when it comes to meeting strangers—but whatever she thought, she kept it to herself.

But Mrs. Morrison had a few minutes' talk with Mrs. Trask one day when I was delayed upstairs, looking for Kim's plastic fish. It was just an old bath toy, but Kim had taken a sudden attachment to it and wouldn't settle down for her nap without it. In the meantime, Mrs. Morrison showed Mrs. Trask around the garden. I could see the two of them from Kim's window, standing chatting by the long side bed of phlox and blue asters—Mrs. Morrison barefoot and casual with tousled hair, Mrs. Trask composed and formal looking, despite what she called her old clothes.

The next day Mrs. Morrison said, "That's a very impressive lady, you know—your Mrs. Trask. Who *is* she, anyway? What's she like as a teacher? And how did you happen to meet her in the first place?"

I chose the last of these questions, and explained, adding, "Though I still don't know how she could tell much about me, just from watching me hit against the backboard."

"Well, I suppose if you have an experienced eye. . . . And apparently she was right about your talent. Oh, she's very guarded in what she says about you"

—Mrs. Morrison grinned at me, seeing I was dying to know—"but I gather she considers you . . . promising. From Mrs. Trask, that's practically a rave, I imagine. Doesn't she ever take off those dark glasses?"

I shook my head. "I think there's something wrong with her eyes."

"Well, does she play herself? Or how do you manage?"

I told her about Mrs. Trask acting as a human target. "And now that I'm working on my serve, well, I just try to put the ball exactly where she says. Not that I can, very often. But I guess it's good practice."

"I should think it might be. You're really working at this, aren't you, Dulcie?" She looked at me thoughtfully. "It must be a long day for you—the job here, and then tennis, and then your chores at home."

I said simply, "It's worth it."

The phone rang, and Mrs. Morrison put a hand out to it; but before she picked it up she said slowly, still staring at me, "Hey—wouldn't it be something if you were really *good* someday, Dulcie? One of the top players, a pro? And I can say I knew you when. . . ."

But of course for the time being, *when* was taking care of her two little girls—back and forth to the playground, the pool, the house; making sandwiches, mopping up spills, reading stories; coaxing Kim out of her occasional tears and Molly out of the rages she sometimes flew into, usually when she was tired.

It was hard to slow Molly down, except by interesting her in some quiet project like crayoning or pasting. One day she found that Kim had messed up her favorite coloring book—just a few stray marks here and there, but according to Molly the book was ruined—and in her fury, she picked up a metal paint box and threw it at her little sister. It caught Kim on the side of the head, just breaking the skin—a small scratch, but it bled a lot, as scalp wounds do.

Molly went white at the sight of the blood and ran out of the house. I felt sort of sick and shaky myself, not because the wound was serious in itself, but because it reminded me of the thing I was always trying to forget. . . . As soon as I'd patched Kim up, I went outside to call Molly, but there was no answer. Mrs. Morrison was off somewhere, and I couldn't leave Kim alone. I wound up dragging her over half the neighborhood, crying and protesting every step of the way, before we finally found Molly hiding in somebody's garage, sure that she'd murdered her little sister.

"Molly, look," I said, pushing Kim forward. "Kim's perfectly all right."

Kim began to cry louder than ever. "Hurts!" she wailed, putting her hand to her head. "Bad Molly!"

Molly looked at her critically; then, with a complete change of mood, said, "Oh, she's just making it up now," and scrambled out into the sunlight. "Shut up, Kim," she ordered, and to my amazement, Kim did.

By the time Mrs. Trask came to pick me up that day, I was feeling pretty beat. When I thought she wasn't looking, I put my head back against the seat for a moment and closed my eyes. But Mrs. Trask didn't miss much. As she swung the car onto Wagon Hill Road, she said, "Bad morning, Dulcie?"

"Oh, the kids got to fighting, that's all."

"Normal enough," Mrs. Trask remarked drily. "Between sisters. Or brothers, for that matter."

"I don't know. My sister and I never fought very much when we were little. I guess we were lucky."

Lucky—and careful, I thought. After what happened —after I was old enough to understand what had happened. . . .

"You've probably just forgotten," Mrs. Trask said with a smile. Then, in a different tone: "About your sister, Dulcie . . ."

She paused, and I came alert. It was unusual for Mrs. Trask to talk about personal things. And what was this about Pat?

Her eyes on the road, Mrs. Trask said, "Mrs. Morrison tells me she's considered quite a tennis player locally. Junior tournaments, and so forth."

"Well, yes. Of course she's not a junior any more. I mean, the competition's a lot harder now." Mixed with my unreasonable anger at Mrs. Morrison—why shouldn't she have mentioned Pat, after all?—was the realization that Pat hadn't actually gotten to the finals very often since she'd graduated to ladies' tennis.

"I see." Mrs. Trask slowed down to avoid a pothole. After a moment she said thoughtfully, "I'd wondered why your parents hadn't bothered to get in touch with me, but perhaps that explains it. . . . Well, all in good time," she added, as if to herself. Then she glanced over at me and asked abruptly: "Can you beat her?"

"Pat?" I must have looked startled; somehow the question had never occurred to me. "Well, I never used to be able to, and we haven't played each other in a long time. So—I don't know."

"I think you ought to find out."

We were turning into the driveway by then, and whatever I might have said was drowned out by Stuart Carter, who came running over from the farmhouse to announce breathlessly that one of their dogs had had puppies that morning. Did we know anyone who wanted a puppy? Because even if they weren't purebred, they were awfully cute, and the father just might have been a golden retriever, which was a good breed, and didn't we want to see them for just a minute?

"Later, Stuart," Mrs. Trask told him firmly. "Right now Dulcie and I have work to do."

ten

MRS. TRASK'S daughter Kate arrived with her children for a two-week stay, and my coaching sessions changed to include some actual play. There was still a good deal of drill, but now it was Kate who patiently hit the ball back to me over and over again while her mother gave directions from the sideline and watched critically. Then we'd play a set or two, with Mrs. Trask stopping us from time to time to analyze strategy and make suggestions. Usually I won fairly easily.

"Wow!" Kate said after one of these sessions, mopping her red face. "This is what I need, all right, I put on so much weight before Peter was born—but I'm not giving you much competition, Dulcie."

153

"You're the perfect practice partner for Dulcie at the moment," her mother told her. "You make so many mistakes."

I thought this sounded pretty harsh, but Kate just grinned and said, "And Dulcie's learning to take advantage of them, right?" She was tall and square-faced like her father, with a calm good humor that I felt was more genuine than his jovial manner.

"Right," said Mrs. Trask. She turned to me. "You ought to be beating Kate 6–1 or even love, Dulcie, not 6–3 and 6–4. I want you to vary the pace of your shots more. Make her run."

"Good heavens!" said Kate. "What do you think I'm doing now? I must have lost five pounds just since I've been here. Not that I mind."

"And don't let her lob," Mrs. Trask went on, ignoring her. "That's the one shot she's smart about. If you can't hit a winner at the net, at least send the ball to her backhand. She'll lob anyway, but it won't be as deep, and you may have a chance at an overhead."

I nodded. We'd been working a lot on overheads, using the same swing I'd learned for my serve. I'd had a tendency to swat at the ball, or even jump for it, compensating for my lack of height, but Mrs. Trask taught me to keep my feet firmly planted. "It's timing that counts," she said, "and control. You want to hit the ball solidly, and usually you'll have plenty of time to get set for an overhead. Make the most of it, and concentrate. There's nothing sadder in tennis than a smash hit into the net."

Now, as Kate went off to check on the baby in his carriage and to collect little Jonathan from the Carters, where Laurie was keeping an eye on him, Mrs. Trask said with a frown: "We've got to line up a regular practice partner for you, Dulcie—for the fall and winter." At my look of surprise, she smiled and said, "There are such things as indoor courts, you know. But never mind that for now, we'll talk about it later. What about a partner, though? I'll want you to go on playing regular sets after Kates leaves. We need someone who plays a good steady game and hits the ball fairly hard. Any ideas?"

I said, "Well, there's my friend Amy. . . ." Amy was getting home from camp next weekend. But then I shook my head. "I guess she's not really good enough, though," I said, and realized sadly that it was true. With what I'd learned this summer, Amy just wouldn't be competition for me any more.

"What was the name of that boy—the one I had you play that day at the recreation center? Mark something. But no, I don't think so." She shook her head dismissively before I could protest. Mark Leonard as a tame practice partner—that would really be the day! "He's not consistent enough, and I doubt if he'd be reliable. I just don't know enough about the local players. Maybe I ought to do some tournament-hopping next weekend."

She looked at her watch and then up at the sky, where a cloud mass was moving in across the sun. "I know it's time we stopped, Dulcie, but we never did work on that backhand volley of yours, and the forecast is for rain tomorrow. Could you stay another twenty minutes or so?"

I hesitated. "I'd like to, but—well, I don't think I'd better, Mrs. Trask. We're having lasagna for supper, and I have to start the sauce."

Mrs. Trask's expression behind the dark glasses was unreadable; she said lightly, "Sauce does come in cans, you know. And some of the mixes aren't bad." She smiled at my horrified face. "All right, Dulcie, but can't someone else do the cooking once in a while?"

"Oh, my sister does sometimes. You know, special things she likes to cook. And every once in a while my Mom gets inspired and makes jam or applesauce, stuff like that. But I enjoy cooking, Mrs. Trask, I really do. And I make good lasagna."

"I'm sure you do."

She seemed about to say something more, but then just shook her head and walked over to let down the tennis net, while I gathered up balls and tossed them into the bucket. The old horse Sally began her slow meander from the far side of the field, knowing I could always be persuaded to give her a handful of grass as we left. It was the same old grass she ate all the time anyway, but I guess having somebody pick it for her made it taste different.

Amy got home from camp with a new shoulder-length haircut and a boyfriend. His name was Rick, and he lived about two hundred miles away in New Hampshire. I figured the romance wouldn't last long if it had to depend on the U.S. mails—knowing what kind of letter writer Amy was—but of course in the meantime I had to hear all about him. I'd been bursting to tell Amy about my summer, all about Mrs. Trask and tennis and my job with the Morrisons, but now I began to wonder if she'd even be interested.

When she'd exhausted the subject of Rick, Amy ruffled up the ends of her hair—it's a super kind of auburn color, and almost makes up for the fact that she can never really get a tan—and said I ought to have mine cut, it was the new length.

"Everybody at camp cut theirs. In fact we all took turns doing each other's. In the middle of the night, by flashlight," Amy said dramatically, and then giggled. "You should have seen some of the kids in the morning! Our counselor practically fainted from shock. Then she got the scissors and finished the trimming herself—I mean, what else could she do? . . . You should get yours cut, Dulcie," she urged me again. "It would look really neat on you."

But I said I didn't want it getting in my face, and my hair was better long so I could tie it back out of the way. "For playing tennis," I explained, in an important voice I immediately despised myself for. "I mean, you want to look good on the court, but you have to be practical, too."

Amy said, well, yes, and didn't I love the new colored tennis dresses; she'd seen a picture of Chris Evert in this nifty peach-colored outfit . . . and then she stared at me and said, what were we talking about, anyway?

So I told her, and she got all excited and wanted to know the details. What was Mrs. Trask like, and what did I mean by drill, and did I really have all these other people turning up just to hit the ball to me so I could practice?

"Wow, that sounds practically professional!" she exclaimed. "Does she tell you what to eat, too, and how much sleep to get, and all that?"

I laughed and said no, not yet. I could see that in Amy's mind I was already jetting around the globe with the other celebrities, my tennis rackets in mink-lined cases, probably.

"Well, what about tournaments and stuff? I mean, when do you *start?*"

I'd wondered about that myself. I knew I wasn't ready yet, but when I was? . . . Mrs. Trask didn't seem to think much of junior tennis, except for certain big tournaments, so I supposed I'd be entering the ladies' division when the time came. But wasn't there an age limit? And was she thinking about the local country club tournaments for a start, or something bigger? I didn't know. So far we'd never really talked about the future. Maybe Mrs. Trask was still making up her mind about me, I thought; and cautioned myself not to get carried away by Amy's enthusiasm.

"Hey," Amy breathed, widening her big hazel eyes at me, "what about Pat? I mean, what if you should meet her in the finals of some big tournament someday? Just think of it! Two sisters," she enlarged, "a fight to the finish, and the parents just sitting there. . . . Gosh, how *would* your parents feel?"

I told her for Pete's sake not to start talking about all this stuff to my parents, or to Pat—that they hadn't really seen me play since Mrs. Trask began coaching me, and that she'd talk to them when she was ready. In fact, I more or less swore Amy to secrecy about our whole conversation, which I knew would appeal to her dramatic sense.

"But still," she said, with her nutty giggle, "you and Pat—can't you just hear the poor umpire? 'Games are 4–3, Miss Kane leads.' Or 'Advantage, Miss Kane.' Wild! Hey, do you think I could come along with you someday—out to this place where you play?"

I shook my head. "Mrs. Trask says no distractions." She hadn't, actually, not in so many words; but I could just imagine how she'd react to having Amy bouncing up and down on the sidelines.

"Yes, okay." Amy was impressed. "But listen, the first big match you play, Dulcie Kane, I get to sit right up front in a box seat!" She pulled a wistful face. "Hey, maybe I could even hold your towel. . . ."

Just having Amy home cheered me up a lot. I guess the summer had been more of a strain than I'd realized. It was hard sometimes, trying to keep the parts of my life separate from one another, concentrating on each part in turn from day to day. With Amy I felt more in one piece—more together, as she'd say.

Then something happened that threatened to pull me apart again. Kate was late for our practice session one day—she'd gone downtown to get a prescription filled for the baby, who had a summer cold. Mrs. Trask and I went on out to the court, taking Stuart Carter along to keep an eye on little Jonathan, Kate's two-year-old. Jonathan had his dump truck to play with, but he was much more fascinated by Sally, the horse. The fascination wasn't mutual. Sally would let him get just so close, and then move away to crop at another patch of grass, keeping a wary eye on her pursuer.

Jonathan thought this was a great game, especially when Sally got impatient enough to move into a trot. He'd shout with laughter and go marching after her again on his short, sturdy legs, calling, "Horsey, horsey!" Stuart followed after him patiently, waiting for him to get tired and go back to his dump truck.

Mrs. Trask and I were doing a kind of warm-up that's also good practice for drop shots—standing on the service line and flicking the ball back and forth to

160

each other, always keeping it within one of the two service courts. She'd just said, "Well, that's enough of that, let's do some work on your serve," when Jonathan set up a terrible screaming from the far end of the field.

I saw Stuart running toward him, and in an instant, I was out the gate and pounding across the uneven stubble to where Jonathan stood bawling at the sky, red-faced and hysterical with fear and pain. My first thought was that he'd gotten too close to the horse and been nipped for his pains; but old Sally was standing some distance away under a clump of trees, watching him with her ears pricked forward, her interest captured at last.

"I think maybe be got stung by a bee," Stuart told me, trying vainly to comfort the little boy.

I squatted down and said, "Oh, poor Jonathan. Show me where it hurts, okay?"

Still yelling, his eyes screwed shut, Jonathan shakily held out his left arm. Sure enough, in the tender flesh inside his elbow, a white welt was rising around the tiny puncture of a bee sting.

I checked to make sure there was no stinger, and and said, "Hey, that hurts, doesn't it, Jonathan? And it was scary too." Jonathan nodded, tears streaming. "But never mind, we'll make it feel better."

Stuart said, "We could put some mud on it," and looked doubtfully around at the hard-baked earth of the field.

161

"Ice would be better," I told him. "Could you run to the house and get some, Stuart? Just wrap up a couple of cubes in a dishtowel or a handkerchief or something."

Stuart dashed away importantly, and I started to pick Jonathan up. But he didn't want to be carried. He struggled, crying harder, so I set him down and took his hand; and together we made our way slowly back toward the tennis court. "Look," I said, "Sally's following us. She wants to make sure you're all right." Jonathan looked around tearfully at the old horse, who was plodding along behind us, and his sobs diminished a little.

"It's okay," I called to Mrs. Trask, who had come partway out into the field. "A bee stung him. He's scared, more than anything else."

"Well, that's a relief! I thought he'd broken his arm, at the very least." She gave Jonathan a hug and said, "That was a nasty old bee, wasn't it, Jon? You come sit down on the bench with us, and let's see if I can find a little treat for you."

"Mommy," Jonathan said, looking around.

"Mommy will be back soon." Mrs. Trask felt around in her handbag and came up with a box of gumdrops. "Standard equipment for grandmothers," she told me, and settled the little boy on the wide wooden bench amid the racket covers and towels and empty tennis ball cans. He sat there sucking a gumdrop obediently, but he looked so small and woebegone that after a moment I pushed some of the gear aside and sat down next to him.

Stuart came back with the ice knotted up in a frayed linen napkin—somehow that was typical of the Carters—and I pressed it gently against the sting, which was swollen now and red around the edges. Jonathan cried a little at first, but then, as the cold numbed the pain, he subsided into long, quavering sighs, his small chest heaving. After a while he relaxed against me, eyelids drooping.

"You're a brave boy," I said, smiling down at him.

Mrs. Trask glanced at her watch impatiently. "I can't imagine what's taking Kate so long. . . . Dulcie, let Stuart sit with Jonathan, and let's get back to work."

I hesitated. "Well, he's calmed down now. Maybe I should stay with him just another minute or two. I mean, it's probably the first time he's ever been stung . . ."

"He'll have forgotten about the whole thing in another fifteen minutes. For heaven's sake, Dulcie, Stuart can manage just as well as you can."

I started to get up, and Stuart moved forward awkwardly. Immediately Jonathan began whimpering and asking for his mother. I turned back to him, and Mrs. Trask's voice cut the air behind me.

"Dulcie! You are here to play tennis, not to act as a nursemaid. On the court, please!"

I had never seen her angry before. She stood with her hands on her hips, her face set and hard. I stared at her, and then reached slowly for my tennis racket.

"Mother!"

Kate came hurrying toward us, looking apologetic. Jonathan set up a wail and held out his arm as if the bee had just now stung him. There were explanations and apologies. Saying she had a salve that was magic for bee stings, and she'd be back in a few minutes, Kate gathered up her son and bore him away. Stuart went with them.

All at once it was so quiet you could hear the thump of an apple falling to the ground in the orchard, and all the August insects shrilling in the grass.

Without looking at Mrs. Trask, I moved onto the court.

"No," she said. "Sit down, Dulcie. I'm sorry I got angry with you just now, but I think it's time we had a talk."

Her voice was calm again. As I walked back to the bench I planned what I would say: He's just a little boy, Mrs. Trask, I didn't think a few minutes mattered so much. Really, it wasn't that I didn't want to play tennis, it was only . . .

But to my surprise, what Mrs. Trask said was, "I saw your sister Pat last weekend, Dulcie. Playing in that tournament over in Westchester. How did she get the scar?"

I stiffened. No one ever mentioned Pat's scar. We never talked about it at home and, of course, old friends knew the story. New ones didn't ask. I said carefully, "It was an accident, when she was little. She—she got cut by a piece of glass."

"How did it happen?"

Mrs. Trask asked the question so directly and matter-of-factly, simply wanting to know, that I found myself able to answer her in almost the same tone.

"I threw a jelly glass at her when I was a baby. She had some toy I wanted, and I was sitting in my high chair, and—I guess the glass had a crack in it to begin with. Anyway, it hit her in the face and broke."

I had a funny sort of hollow feeling as I spoke the words—the first time I had ever said them to anybody. They were my mother's words, really, not mine. The seventeen stiches; the plastic surgeons who had done all they could, then or probably ever. . . . I had no memory of any of it, only what I'd been told, and my own imagination. That was enough. I felt the hot tears squeezing themselves against my eyelids.

Mrs. Trask nodded thoughtfully, as if I'd confirmed something she had already guessed. She didn't offer any words of comfort, or talk about how accidents will happen, the best thing is to forget—any of the things my parents had said. Instead she said slowly, as if she were choosing her words, "Pat isn't really a good tennis player, Dulcie. You know that, don't you? Even with good coaching, she could never be more than a fair club player. Not like you. You can be first-rate, if you want to be."

I started to speak, but she shook her head. "Oh, I know you can work, Dulcie, you've proved that. But what about the rest of your life? If you go on with this, you know, there are a great many things you'll have to give up. And I don't mean just all the time involved—all the hours you'll be spending on a tennis court, when you could be having fun with your friends or going out on dates, or just loafing. Some of your feelings will have to take second place, too. About Pat, for instance."

"But tennis matters to her!" I blurted. "She . . ."

"No!" Mrs. Trask said sharply. "Not the way it does to you. You're a winner, Dulcie. At least I think you are. But it's not enough to win on the court. You have to win a place for yourself as a person too. That means you've got to stop sacrificing your own life for Pat's, to begin with." She held up a hand to silence my protest. "Whatever you owe her, you've paid back long ago. That's something I hope you'll realize for yourself one of these days. But never mind Pat for now. Dulcie, you've simply got to stop trying to *please* people all of the time! Sometimes you'll have to hurt them or disappoint them or make them angry, to get where you want to be."

She paused, and then said evenly, "In terms of tennis, that means you can take the court against your best friend, in front of a big gallery, let's say, and not give an inch, not one single point, not even if you're beating her six–love in straight sets. Do you understand what I'm saying?"

I said slowly, "It sounds like . . . well, kind of a hard way to be."

"Hard, and ruthless sometimes." She smiled a little at my expression. "I don't mean you have to turn yourself into a monster, Dulcie, just that you have to learn to make choices. I've known some successful people in my time, people who made it to the top, and they all had one thing in common: when it came to a choice between doing their thing, as you kids put it, and doing what someone else thought they should do, they didn't have to think twice. I suppose that's what you call being professional—in sports or any other field."

She looked down at her clasped hands, and I saw her fingers tighten, the knuckles going white. Her wedding band flashed in the sun.

She said quietly, "I made a choice once, Dulcie, and I've never been sure it was the right one. Oh, I know, grown-ups are supposed to be sure, but you'd be surprised how many of them aren't. . . ."

She paused. "At any rate, I was a good tennis player once. My coach even thought I could be the best, given time and experience, and so did quite a few other people. But I fell in love, and it was wartime, and right then nothing seemed more important than getting married. Oh, I was planning to go on playing tennis; but then my husband was posted overseas, and I had a chance to be near him, and pretty soon there was a baby on the way. Even so, I was still young. I thought when the baby was a few months old, I could start getting back into shape and take up where I'd left off. The war was ending by then, and . . ."

She sighed. "Tennis was different in those days, as perhaps you know. It was all amateur, at least for the women, and unless you had some independent means of support . . . well, there was no financial security in it, to put it mildly. So if you had a husband and child, and all the responsibilities that went with them. . . . I did play in a couple of tournaments after the war," she said wryly, "and I was terrible. I think now it was because I was so divided in my own mind, feeling guilty and confused and not really knowing what I wanted. But I lost confidence in myself on the court, and that was that; or so it seemed. Anyway, I had another baby, and then another, and"—she turned to smile at me, a real smile now—"lived more or less happily ever after."

I said stupidly, "Then, it wasn't because of your eyes?"

"My eyes?" Mrs. Trask raised a hand to her dark glasses, looking puzzled. Then she burst out laughing. "Oh, Dulcie, is that what you thought? I should have explained. I had a cataract operation last spring, and that's why I have have to wear these things. Someday I'll be able to get rid of them, or at least exchange them for a lighter pair. The operation was only partially successful, but . . ." She shrugged. "I guess I'm lucky at that."

I sat staring down at the blur of my racket strings, feeling sad for Mrs. Trask—sad, and angry, too. She hadn't said a word against her husband, but I could imagine well enough what Mr. Trask's attitude would have been, even as a young man. *His* wife wasn't going to go traipsing off from one tennis tournament to another while he stayed meekly at home. Never mind how many titles she won—tennis was only a game, after all; and he certainly couldn't be expected to make beds or change a diaper or cook his own dinner. . . .

Mrs. Trask gave my shoulder a little shake. "Don't look so gloomy, Dulcie. I did what I wanted, I think, in the long run. Most people do. But it's always bothered me a little that I didn't really choose. I just took the course of least resistance, in a way; even if it turned out to be the right one for me. In other words, I drifted." It was hard to imagine Mrs. Trask drifting. My face must have shown my disbelief, because she said, "Most women did, you know. I'm afraid most of them still do."

"That's what Pat says," I told her; and wondered fleetingly if she was thinking of her daughter Andrea, the one who seemed to be drifting into marriage.

"Does she?" Mrs. Trask smiled. "I'd like to meet Pat. But anyway, Dulcie, the point is that things have changed, and especially in the world of tennis. It can be a real career now, you know. There's money to be made, even for women, with tennis such big business; in fact, a good head for business is almost as much of an asset these days as a good backhand. It's still a hard life, but now at least there are practical rewards. So maybe I didn't really have much of a choice, Dulcie; but you will."

Kate was coming back, pushing the baby carriage carefully over the grass. Mrs. Trask got to her feet and stood looking down at me.

"Don't misunderstand me, Dulcie. I'm not saying you can't combine a tennis career with marriage and a family eventually—lots of women do, though it can't be easy for them. But if you're serious about tennis, you've got to get your priorities straight in your own mind, starting now."

When I was silent, feeling confused and rather overwhelmed, she said gently, "I know. Thirteen's pretty young to be deciding on a career. But that's the way it is, I'm afraid, if you want to make it to the top. You have to make the commitment now. Otherwise, no matter how hard you work, you'll just be cheating yourself." She sighed. "As it is, there'll be all kinds of pressures on you; but the sooner you let other people know you mean business, the easier you'll make things for yourself. Even so, some of your friends at school, for instance, are going to think you're pretty peculiar, even something of a freak . . ."

"Oh, I don't mind that," I said, and it was true; that was one of the ways I'd changed over the summer.

"No, I don't think you do. But what about tomato sauce, Dulcie? What about crying children?" She was smiling a little, but her voice was serious. "What if a good friend comes up to you after school someday and says will you please explain the math homework to her because she'll fail if you don't, her parents will ground her and stop her allowance, her whole life will be ruined. . . . Do you just say, 'Sorry, I've got to play tennis now,' and turn away?"

"I'm not all that great at math myself," I said, and we both laughed. But then I shook my head. I just didn't know.

eleven

AND SO the summer ended, and with it my job at the Morrisons'. Kim cried, Molly presented me with a clay dog she'd made—"It was supposed to have been a rabbit," she explained, "but the ears kept falling off"—and Mrs. Morrison said I had a permanent baby-sitting job whenever I wanted it. School began, we had our day at Forest Hills, and still nothing had been arranged about my future. Or so I thought.

Then on Saturday afternoon, my mother said, "Oh, Dulcie, I had a call from your friend Mrs. Trask this morning while you were over at Amy's. She's invited us all over there for a picnic lunch tomorrow, and some tennis if the weather improves." It had been raining off and on all day. "I said fine, we'd love to. . . . What's the matter?"

We were in the family room, where I was making brown-paper covers for my school books; I'd just dropped the scissors with a bang onto the tiled floor. "Nothing. . . . I mean, that's very nice of her. If it doesn't rain."

"Well, let's hope it won't. I'm looking forward to meeting her. In fact, we probably should have asked her here before now"—her face wore the frown it gets at the thought of an unwelcome social obligation—"but heavens, I don't know where the summer went. Anyhow, she said she'd like to meet us, and she's been so nice to you, I thought we ought to go." She added casually, "I wonder if any of the Carters will be around."

"They usually are," I said. So it was really the Carters Mom wanted to meet—the rich, socially-prominent Carter family. Wait till she got a look at the peeling paint, the tangled shrubbery, the old tractor rusting away behind the garage. I suppressed a smile.

Mom said, "I don't suppose the older son— Johnny, is it?—has left for college yet," and I decided I was being unfair. It was Pat she was really thinking of; though what did she expect, some kind of instant romance? . . . But I was hoping Johnny would be on hand, too, for my own sake. Things had a way of being easier when Johnny was around.

My hands shook a little as I fitted paper around my heavy new science book. I told myself it was ridiculous to feel so nervous. But—tomorrow! And my whole family! Why hadn't Mrs. Trask given me some warning? I hadn't heard from her all week. Kate had left last weekend, and Mrs. Trask had said she knew I'd be busy, what with school starting; she'd give me a call soon.

Instead of which, she'd called my mother. I felt angry and somehow betrayed. "All in good time," she'd said. But then I could hear her saying, as clearly as if she'd been in the room with me, "If you won't force the issue, Dulcie, I guess I'll have to."

Later I escaped to the upstairs phone and called Amy.

"Oh, wow! It's the Confrontation at last!" she exclaimed; Amy loves big words. "Oh, Dulcie, I wish I could be there too. I mean, maybe you'll need some moral support, sort of, and—listen, couldn't you say you'd already invited me over for the day? And you couldn't just uninvite me? I wouldn't eat much, I promise."

I had to laugh at that—Amy's appetite is famous in my family. But I was sure Mrs. Trask wouldn't mind one more guest, and just the thought of having Amy along made me feel a lot better. Not that I can lean on her, I reminded myself, thinking of things Mrs. Trask had said; I have to be strong in myself, by myself. Still: "I'll have to check with Mom," I told Amy, "but I'm sure it'll be okay."

"Terrific! Hey"—her voice dropped dramatically—"how do you think she'll manage it? I know, we'll all be sitting around eating our fried chicken or whatever, and then Mrs. Trask will draw your parents aside—like she'll take them into the library—"

"Amy! There isn't any library, and besides, we'll probably be outdoors."

"Well, you know what I mean. And she'll say, "You have a remarkable daughter, Mr. and Mrs. Kane. . . .""

"And they'll say, 'Which one?' " I was surprised at the bitterness in my own voice.

"Oh, Dulcie! See, you really do need me to come along. Go ask your Mom right now."

I did, and it was okay, but nothing else turned out the way either Amy or I expected.

In the first place, there was the business of Eric and the Carters' puppies. Stuart was out playing with them on the overgrown front lawn of the farmhouse when we pulled into the driveway at noon the next day. Before you could say Jack Robinson—or golden retriever; the puppies *were* sort of a gold color—Eric was out of the car and streaking across to join the fray. In another moment he was down on the grass tussling with the puppies and probably getting grass stains on the good white shirt Mom had insisted he wear.

"Eric!" Dad called sharply. "Come back here!"

But you couldn't even see Eric for the puppies.

"Dulcie, go bring him back, will you?" My mother gave a sigh as she got out of the car. "You

175

ought to have warned me. Eric just seems to have a screw loose when it comes to dogs."

As a matter of fact, it had been on the tip of my tongue a dozen times to tell them about the puppies, and to beg them to let Eric have one. But all I said was, "Maybe you should let him get it out of his system," and went off to try and pry Eric away. Pry was the word, too. By then Eric was lying on his back with one puppy nibbling at his ear, another tugging at his shoelaces, and a third scrabbling around on his chest. He smiled up at me rapturously and said, "Aren't they *nice,* Dulcie?"

Stuart was breathlessly trying to round up the other three. He said, "Well, we've got to find homes for them soon. You should see what they're doing to the house inside. Mom says we may have to get a whole new kitchen floor. Hey! Come back here, you!" He went charging off after a puppy that was making for the road.

So I missed seeing the initial meeting between my parents and Mrs. Trask. By the time I got Eric away—"yes, I'll talk to Mom and Dad, but *later,* Eric, and don't get your hopes up"—everyone else had gone inside. Mr. Trask was showing my parents and Amy around the house, explaining details of how the old barn had been converted, and Mrs. Trask had Pat helping her in the kitchen—trying to put her at her ease, I realized. Pat had dithered around all morning, mainly about what to wear, and had almost changed her mind about coming at the last minute. I thought she looked great in a pale green shirt and beige mini-skirt that showed off her long tanned legs; but I could tell by the way she held her head turned a little away from Mrs. Trask as she helped set a tray that she still felt self-conscious.

After a while everybody moved out onto the small back terrace, which was sheltered from the wind by a brick wall along two sides. The sun had come out, but the day was cool and breezy—a fall day, full of flickering cloud shadows, and the first leaves falling.

The conversation during lunch was general, with no talk of tennis except for some speculation about the finals at Forest Hills, which were to be shown on TV later that afternoon. Pat said she hoped Evonne Goolagong would win the women's title, she was tired of watching Billie Jean King walk away with everything, and Amy said Billie Jean fought for everything she got and deserved to win. They glared at each other, and Dad laughed and said something about feminist in-fighting, and then they both glared at *him*.

Still it was all so relaxed and pleasant that I almost forgot to be nervous, and there was more than enough food to go around—including the macaroni and cheese casserole Amy ate most of. She gave me a significant look from time to time, between mouthfuls, but I pretended not to notice. Mrs. Trask had wanted to meet my family; maybe that was all there was to it, at least for today.

The grown-ups were drinking their coffee when Mom noticed that Eric had disappeared.

"Oh, for heaven's sake! I suppose he's back playing with all those dogs again. Dulcie, go find him, will you? Tell him he can have another piece of cake if he wants it."

"He's over in the orchard," Mrs. Trask said calmly. "I told him to see how many windfalls he could collect. The apples are small and rather wormy, I'm afraid, but they make good applesauce."

Mom still looked worried. "Well—I don't want him disturbing the Carters. Dulcie, I'd feel better if you'd go check on him. He's probably climbing the trees by now. You know Eric."

I did, and also that Eric could climb like a monkey. But I stood up automatically to obey.

Mrs. Trask set down her coffee cup with a deliberate little click. She said, "I thought we'd all go over that way in a minute anyhow, to the tennis court. You did bring tennis things, I hope?"

Amy said quickly, "I'll go check on Eric, Mrs. Kane," and left the terrace before my mother could say anything.

Dad said, "Tennis, after all that good food?" He stretched and patted an imaginary paunch.

"We'll let the young play first," Mrs. Trask told him, with a smile. "Besides, I'd like you to see some of the work I've been doing with Dulcie this summer. Maybe Pat would give her a game. How about it?" She turned to Pat. "Will you two play some singles while the rest of us recover from lunch?"

It was all done so smoothly that no one but me had any idea what she was up to. I was glad Amy wasn't there. Pat shrugged and said, "Well, sure," and Mom said had we brought our tennis dresses?— knowing we had, because she herself had insisted on it. I was not going to play tennis at the Carters' in my crumby old shirt and shorts, she said, ignoring the fact that I'd been doing just that all summer.

We all went into the house to change, using various bedrooms. I could hear my mother exclaiming to Mrs. Trask about how immaculate the house was, saying she was no housekeeper herself, and she didn't know what she'd do without me. "Dulcie's a born housewife—so efficient, and it all seems so *effortless* for her. . . ."

In the guest room where Pat and I were changing, we exchanged our usual grimace at this; but my heart wasn't in it. What on earth *was* Mom going to do without me, I wondered. Because if I embarked on the kind of tennis schedule Mrs. Trask seemed to have in mind, somebody else was going to have to mop floors and do the ironing, to say nothing of the cooking. Pat? But I couldn't look at Pat, who was calmly adjusting her headband in front of the mirror, obviously resigned to playing a boring set or two with her younger sister, and maybe hoping Johnny Carter would show up to admire her form on the court.

To distract myself, I looked at a framed photograph on the bedtable. Andrea, this must be, the younger daughter I knew Mrs. Trask worried about. She was startlingly pretty, almost beautiful, except for something sulky and discontented about her eyes and mouth. Drifting into marriage—was she? I thought that must be about the worst kind of drifting you could do, and suddenly I felt grateful for my own parents. Whatever their faults, I knew they were committed to each other and to us. Even if Mom didn't like housework.

Pat and I walked out to the tennis court ahead of the others, taking the familiar path through the grape arbor and the apple orchard. The air smelled spicy with ripened fruit, and now you really had to watch out for yellowjackets. There was no sign of Eric or Amy until we reached the field. Then we both stopped dead at the sight of Amy leading the old brown horse around in a circle with Eric sitting proudly astride.

"Amy!" I yelled.

"Oh, good grief," said Pat. "Mom will have a fit."

"It's okay," Amy called back. "Johnny said we could." I saw her do a double take at the two of us in our tennis clothes; but all she said was, "It's kind of windy for tennis, isn't it?" and moved off, Sally plodding at her heels.

It was windy, out here in the open, and the wind would be in my favor, I thought. No matter how poorly I played, I knew I could hit the ball a lot harder than Pat, and also I knew that the wind would affect her serve more than it would mine. But I didn't underestimate Pat's game. I knew how controlled and steady she was, and that I couldn't afford to make many mistakes.

"Does Amy know anything about horses?" Pat was looking after them.

"Oh, sure, she's ridden a lot at camp. Besides, Sally's very gentle."

"Gentle, meaning lazy," said Johnny Carter, startling us both. He rose from a squatting position inside the corner of the court, where he'd been making some repairs to the fence with a roll of wire. He stuck a pair of wire cutters in his back pocket and strolled over to us as we let ourselves in the gate.

"Hi, Dulcie. And you're Pat—I remember." Pat nodded stiffly. "And that wild man out there must be your brother. He says he's going to be a jockey."

I smiled. "Well, that's a new one. Yesterday he wanted to be a vet."

"Not that he even knows what a vet does," Pat said, with her scornful laugh. "He thinks it's a matter of handing out dog biscuits and maybe bandaging a sore paw once in a while."

But Johnny said seriously, "I was the same way when I was little. I wanted to be a doctor and make people well—you know. Then I broke my arm and spent an afternoon in the emergency room, and that was the end of my medical career. Real blood—I mean, that was just too much." He gave us his great smile and said, "Well, I'll see you later. I promised Mom I'd cut the grass today, only nobody told me I'd have to fix the mower first. If you hear curses followed by an explosion, that'll be me."

I knew Johnny did have to cut the grass—we could hear the mower sputtering and growling in the distance as we were warming up—but I think he also sensed the tension I was feeling and decided we'd be better off without him as a spectator. As I said before, that's the way Johnny is: able to take in an entire situation at a glance.

But Pat—well, I don't know just when Pat began to take in what was happening. I won the first set 6–2, and I really don't think she even realized she was in trouble until I'd taken her serve twice and was serving at 4–2. She tried some desperation lobbing then, to drive me away from the net, but all the running I'd done for Mrs. Trask stood me in good stead. I got the lobs back, and on my next shot was usually able to take the net again, or at least force Pat out of position enough to hit the ball cross-court for a winner.

Our gallery had grown silent during the last few

games. Mr. Trask had stayed behind to finish some chores at the house, but my parents and Mrs. Trask were sitting on the bench, and Amy had flopped down on the grass outside the fence after letting old Sally loose. At first they'd all been laughing and chatting among themselves, with Dad calling out, "Attaway, slugger!" when I whammed back a service return or put away a volley. I heard my mother say to Mrs. Trask, "Goodness, Dulcie certainly has improved, hasn't she? I can see you've helped her a lot with her serve. I think she was throwing the ball too high before."

I had to smile at that—it was true enough, but what a way to describe all the thought and labor that had gone into my reconstructed serve!

But by that last game, I didn't feel like smiling; no one did, not even Amy. Pat was down 2–5, and had to win her serve. Instead she fell apart. Three double faults in a row, and then a fluky soft serve to my backhand. I returned it poorly, and all Pat had to do was hit the ball down the line—but she sent it into the net.

She stood shaking her head and trying to laugh. "Ouch!" she said. "That hurt." She looked at me across the net and said, "You want to play another?"

"Sure," I said quickly. I wanted to add something about how she wasn't really warmed up yet—which was true, in a way, because she certainly hadn't expected to have to work for each point. No one likes to win the way I just had, and I knew she could play much better tennis. But I was afraid anything I said might come out sounding wrong, so I turned and picked up a ball and walked back to the baseline to serve.

"Unless someone else wants to play? . . ."

Pat looked politely at Mrs. Trask, who shook her head and said, no, there was plenty of time, we'd have some doubles later on. In fact the whole first set had taken only about fifteen minutes.

I won my serve, but just barely. Pat was concentrating now, and fighting back with everything she had. In fact of the two of us, I was the shakier. I couldn't seem to get my first serve in all of a sudden, and I still didn't have much of a second serve—that was something Mrs. Trask wanted to start working on soon. I had to wait my chance to go in to the net, and with Pat placing those long graceful ground strokes of hers carefully and accurately, it was hard to find an opening. The score went to deuce and back several times. Finally I won the game on a high backhand volley, almost a smash, that I have to admit was a spectacular shot. It hit the tape in the corner and bounced into the fence with a high ringing sound.

Pat stood biting her lip. She was almost in tears, too upset even to congratulate me on the shot—and that in itself was making her feel worse, I knew.

I said, "I was lucky on that one," and saw Mrs. Trask frown. In fact that high volley was a shot we'd practiced a lot. She said with my strong wrist and forearm, it ought to be a real weapon for me, not just a defensive move when there wasn't time to take the volley with my forehand.

As we walked around to the side of the net to change courts, I saw Johnny leave the mower at the edge of the apple orchard and come hurrying over to speak to my mother. She looked alarmed, and then exasperated. I saw her throw an odd, quick, calculating glance at me as she stood up.

"Dulcie, come with me for just a minute, will you? Eric's been stung by a yellowjacket," she explained to the others. "It got him in several places, and he's in the orchard having hysterics and won't come out. Dulcie's the only one who can handle him when he gets like this."

Another bee sting! Remembering little Jonathan, I looked at Mrs. Trask, expecting her to intervene; but she said mildly, "It's been a bad year for yellowjackets. Johnny was mowing under the trees, he must have stirred up a nest."

"We won't be long," my mother said, opening the gate. No one protested. I think we all realized that Pat could use a breather—especially my father, who got up to rally with her while I was gone. Dad knew as well as I did that if Eric really was in hysterics, he was the one who could calm him down the quickest.

But Eric wasn't hysterical; in fact he was trying his hardest not to cry. We found him standing under one of the gnarled old trees next to the basket of apples he'd been collecting, his face tear-stained but stoic. The yellowjacket had got up under his shirt somehow and had stung him on the back in two or three places in its frantic effort to escape.

Mom inspected his bony little shoulder blade for a stinger, then dropped the shirt and gave him a pat. "Do you want me to put something on it?" Eric shook his head. "Well, why don't you take the apples back up to the house now and find something else to do."

"Could I go see the puppies, Mom? I hardly got to see them at all before." His face brightened, he looked at her pleadingly.

"Oh, I guess so. Go see the puppies, Eric, but don't stay too long."

Eric gave a whoop and ran off, forgetting the apples.

I turned to my mother. I guess I already knew what she was going to say.

"All right, Dulcie," she said grimly. "I got you out here because I wanted to talk to you. Do you realize what you're doing to your sister? How you're humiliating her in front of all these people?"

"All what people?" I said; but there was a lump in my throat. "Mrs. Trask just . . ."

"Never mind Mrs. Trask!" she snapped. "I'm talking about you and Pat. Why do you have to hurt her this way?"

"But Mom, I've been working hard on my tennis,

I tried to tell you, and I can't *help* it if I'm better than Pat now! What do you want me to do? I can't just walk away." I could feel the tears rising.

"I want you to let up on her. Oh, I can see you're good, Dulcie, and that's something we'll have to talk about later. I'm not trying to take anything away from you. But right now"—she brought her face close to mine, and I saw how strained and haggard she looked—"you're going back on that court and give Pat some points if you have to. Anything to keep the score from being so lopsided this time."

"It won't be anyway. I mean, Pat's playing better now, and—"

"Dulcie, I'm not asking you to lose to her, I'm asking you to *let up!*"

I stared at her. Then I shook my head. "I'm sorry, but I can't. I can't play that way."

"Then you'll default. You'll develop a cramp or something, and say you have to stop. You've already proved your point, Dulcie, you and Mrs. Trask. You're better than Pat; in a few years you won't even be in the same league with her. But I will not let you go back out there and destroy her! You know what a hard time she's had, and how much her tennis has meant to her—"

"I don't think you're being fair to Pat." It was my turn to interrupt; suddenly I was furiously angry. "She's a lot stronger than that."

"Only because we've tried to support her and

protect her ever since she was hurt."

Hurt by me, I thought; she hadn't said it, but I knew that was what she meant. I put out a hand to the rough bark of the apple tree, feeling as if she'd struck me.

"Oh, Dulcie, don't look like that! It was just an accident, we all know that!" She put her arms around me, but I felt as rigid and hard inside as the tree trunk. "You were only a baby, you didn't mean anything by it. All babies throw things when they get mad, and even at eighteen months you had a good strong left arm. . . ."

I could feel her trying to make me smile, but I didn't look at her.

"Nobody blames you," she went on, "least of all Pat. And now . . . Oh, Dulcie, you know how generous Pat has always been toward you. It just seems to me the least you can do is . . . Where are you going?"

I had broken away from her, I was running down the path.

"Dulcie!"

"I'm going back to play tennis," I shouted at her.

"Dulcie, wait!"

But I didn't wait. I ran on down the grassy path that led to the tennis court, between the trunks of apple trees that were blurred and shining wet with my angry tears.

twelve

MRS. TRASK glanced quickly up at me as I let myself in the gate and looked around for my racket. I kept my head down, but I knew she could tell something was wrong. My mother followed a few moments later, her face tight and composed. She sat down on the bench, hitching up her sweater against the wind that was blowing much harder now, and said with a little laugh that Eric seemed to have survived the yellowjackets after all, and she was sorry we'd been so long.

My father hit a last ball to Pat, and I took his place on the court. As he passed me, he gave me a look of appeal: take it easy on her, can't you? "All yours, Boots," was what he said—but that was more of the same, using my old nickname to remind me of my place in the family: the younger sister, the one you could tease, the pretty, uncomplicated daughter who was always glad to oblige.

For those few minutes I think I actually hated my parents. It's a kind of blackmail, I thought numbly. Maybe in a way they've been blackmailing me all my life. And I've let them get away with it. But if I let them get away with it now, I'm finished—and not just on the tennis court.

Amy was sitting behind me outside the fence, hugging her knees to her chin, her bright hair whipped back by the wind. "Aren't you *cold?*" she asked. And then: "Dulcie, you okay?"

But I didn't want to talk to Amy. Crazily enough, it was Pat I wanted to explain it all to; Pat, who would understand that somehow I had to survive, and that it could only be on my own terms.

She called, "Do you want to hit a few?"

"No. You go ahead and serve."

"Okay. Games are love–one," she announced at large, in proper country club style, and bounced a ball in a quick, confident way before she took her first serve. I could see she'd pulled herself together while I was gone. She was ready now to take me on as a real opponent, forgetting for the moment that I was her younger sister whom she'd beaten so easily over the years.

I wished I could feel the same way. But I was

shaken and upset; the image of Pat's scarred face seemed to keep getting between me and the ball. And now the wind was a real factor. Standing in the deuce court, Pat had it directly behind her, and she served carefully because of it—shortening her toss, not hitting the ball hard for fear the wind would carry it out. As a result, her serve had little momentum of its own. The ball floated and wavered as it came over the net, and the bounce was hard to judge. I had my old trouble with handling a soft ball, and my return landed in the net.

The advantage court wasn't much better. Pat was serving slightly across the path of the wind now, but she still didn't hit the ball hard enough to compensate for its effect. This wasn't deliberate, I knew: Pat just doesn't have a very strong serve, and the more she wants to win, the more cautiously she hits it. The ball bounced short to my forehand, and the wind blew it sideways to my backhand. I managed to return it somehow and went on up to the net—I was almost there anyhow, and I'd hit a fairly deep shot down the center of the court. But I'd reckoned without the wind. Pat had it directly behind her as she took the ball with her forehand, and her passing shot went whistling by me to land six inches inside the baseline.

"Good shot!" I called; and it was, even if the wind did help.

Thirty–love. I returned another serve into the

191

net, won the next point on an error of Pat's—I sent up a lob, of all crazy things to do in that wind, and Pat tried for an overhead and missed—and at 40–15 I hit the serve out, for a change. I'd been so determined to whack the ball this time that I overhit it, taking too much backswing, just as the wind dropped for a moment. Game to Pat.

As I walked back into the corner to retrieve a ball, I glanced over at the grown-ups on the bench. Mrs. Trask shook her head at me, smiling a little. I could hear her saying it: Okay, Dulcie, playing in the wind is murder; *nobody* likes it. Even the pros find their timing thrown off by it, and their bread-and-butter shots going for nothing. The only way to beat the wind is to concentrate. Never take your eye off the ball, not even for a fraction of a second. And use it if you can; make it work for you.

In my case, using the wind meant getting up to the net, hitting short, sharp volleys that wouldn't be affected by it, maybe forcing Pat to try and lob over me. I was thinking about all this as I walked back to serve; and then, belatedly, the expression on my parents' faces registered on me. They looked oddly relieved, almost approving. Why, they actually thought I'd thrown that last game away on purpose! My returns into the net, and that stupid lob. . . .

I stood gripping the handle of my racket so hard that my whole arm trembled. Behind me, Amy said something, but her words were blown away by the wind.

All right, *here goes!* I thought, and tossed the ball up for my first serve.

I threw everything into that serve, including my sense of outrage and shame. They've known me all my life, I thought furiously. Is that really the kind of person they think I am? I flung my racket head at the ball viciously, with all my strength—and I was lucky. The wind was against me, and a serve that would otherwise have gone out by a good two feet hit the service line for an ace.

So much for my strategy. I won the game on straight serves that Pat either missed altogether or returned into the net. I didn't look at Mrs. Trask as we changed sides. I'd been on the verge of losing control, and anyway, win or lose, I knew that had been bad tennis—not really my game at all. My serve was designed primarily to get me up to the net, not to be a weapon in itself. A stronger player would have blasted it right back at me and caught me flat-footed with nowhere to go.

Now it was Pat's turn to serve into the wind. I realized I couldn't afford any more outbursts; I had to settle down and concentrate. But returning her serve was tricky. Sometimes the ball seemed to stop dead in midair, sometimes it wobbled crazily before it bounced and then curved off to one side. I stroked it carefully, literally watching the seam of the ball as my racket made contact, and managed to keep my returns in the court.

But if Pat's serve was weak, she was hitting her

ground strokes hard—harder than I'd ever seen her hit them, I realized, really smacking the ball, as she could safely do with the wind against her. Once the wind dropped just as she was hitting a forehand drive; I halted in my movement toward the ball, and we both stood watching it sail out, a good three feet beyond the baseline. We looked at each other and laughed, and that broke some of the tension.

The score went to 40–30, and then Pat won the game on a long backcourt rally that had everyone applauding, as she finally got a good cross-court angle and put the ball away. I'd been playing too cautiously, I realized, afraid of hitting a forcing shot out, and so not getting up to the net. I'd stayed on the baseline most of the time, putting a lot of topspin on my drives and never really going for a winner, hoping Pat would make the error. But as I've said, Pat's the steady, consistent kind of player who thrives on long rallies, and all I was doing was playing her game.

So, 2–all, and my serve. Two–all! I felt as if we'd been playing for hours. I hadn't looked over at the sidelines except to notice that Johnny had joined our gallery, leaning up against the fence with his arms folded and looking thoughtful. But I wasn't thinking about Johnny, I wasn't even thinking about Pat any more, except as a moving white figure on the other side of the net. My mind was occupied with the problem of the next game: how to serve with the

wind behind me and still give myself time to get up to the net, which was where I knew I wanted to be.

I stood bouncing a ball and wishing I knew more about putting a spin on my serve—what kind to use, and how much, under these conditions. But so far we'd concentrated on a basic flat serve, trying to make it hard and deep and accurate, fast enough so it couldn't be returned easily, but not so fast that I couldn't get to the net behind it. I decided the only thing to do now was slow down my stroke a little and take something off the ball, trusting to the wind to keep it deep.

A really tremendous gust pushed my first serve out. Pat wasn't sure about the bounce, and hit the ball back. "Take two," she called, but I shook my head. I punched my second serve over the net, thought, oh, well, and went charging up after it. Pat was taken by surprise; her return to my forehand was hit hard, but within easy reach, and I slapped it away for the point.

I was able to serve harder into the other court, since the wind wasn't directly behind me, although I had to be careful to hit down on the ball to control its direction. I put it where I wanted, angled wide to Pat's backhand, but she in turn got a good angle on the ball—one of the hazards of a wide serve, as I'd discovered. I leapt to my left and managed to cut off her return: not much of a shot, but at least it stayed in the court. Pat was ready for it and tried to pass me down the deuce-court line, maybe forgetting that her forehand side was mine as well, or maybe figuring I'd be expecting a cross-court shot.

I volleyed the ball deep at an angle into her backhand corner, and that should have been the point—except that Pat somehow covered the distance with those long legs of hers and got off a really beautiful, low, topspin drive to my backhand that was dropping fast as it came over the net. I got my racket on it, but just barely. The ball skidded down the center service line, and again Pat was there somehow, coming up on the run to hit a half-volley to my left and behind me.

Still off-balance from my backhand lunge, I backpedaled, reached, and hit a sort of hip-pocket dink shot that just cleared the net. Pat stayed with it and smacked the ball wide to my forehand. I had to stretch for it from my toes, like a football player making a tackle, but I got the volley somehow. Pat returned it, forehand to forehand, and there we both were, at the net where Pat hates to be, firing volleys at each other like bullets.

But as I've said, that's my game. I had fleeting glimpses of Pat's taut, strained face as we leapt and crouched and spun, but it meant nothing to me. I got the opening I wanted and angled the ball under Pat's backhand for the point.

Our gallery was laughing and clapping. Mr. Trask, who'd just strolled onto the scene, called out,

"Wow! That's some tennis! Is that what you two girls do for relaxation?"

Actually I don't suppose that final exchange at the net amounted to more than five or six shots, but that kind of tennis is always fun to watch. Of course as a player you don't visualize yourself, and you hardly even see the other player; in fact you don't really think much at all about what you're doing—at least I don't. Reflexes take over, I guess, and training.

I felt exhilarated, my whole body tingling and alive. For the moment I'd forgotten this was anything but an ordinary set of tennis. Who cared what the score was? I'd fought for a good point against a stubborn opponent and won it. That was all that mattered.

But there's often a moment in a match you recognize later as having been crucial. The games were still 2–all, and I was only ahead 30–love in this one; but that last point had taken something out of Pat. We grinned at each other as we turned away from the net, but I noticed how her shoulders slumped as she walked back to the baseline, her racket hanging loose in her hand. It was a moment before she squared up to receive serve, looking intent and determined once more. She won the next point on a high lob that the wind held in, but I took the next two with easy put-aways at the net for the game.

She tried. When we changed courts, and it was Pat's turn to serve again with the wind behind her,

198

she stopped poking at the ball and instead took her chances on a hard serve. Sometimes the ball went out, but even when it didn't, she was giving me something I could hit. I was able to go all out on my ground strokes, hitting some of them for winners, following others in to the net. I think Pat realized this, and knew she'd have a better chance of forcing errors from me if she just tapped the ball over the net and let the wind do the rest. But she wouldn't play it that way. If she was going to lose, she was going to do it in style.

What would I have done in her place? Mrs. Trask asked me that later. I thought a moment and said, "Anything to win," and we both laughed. But I wasn't sure.

The score went to 4–2, then 5–2, as I won my serve easily, without giving up a point. During this last game, Mr. Trask—who seemed unaware that anything was at stake between the two of us—kept making enthusiastic comments between points.

"Hey, that was real textbook tennis," he said as we changed sides. "Serve, rush the net, one volley, two volleys, and *pow!* that's it. Yes, Dulcie's really coming along," he told his wife. "I'm beginning to see what you mean about her. Give her a few more inches, a few more pounds—in the right places, hey, Dulcie?—and she'll be sensational."

I smiled politely. Pat's face was expressionless. She looked tired and fine-drawn, her features sharper than usual, which made the scar stand out more. Of course we'd both been doing a lot of running; and now Pat had to serve into the wind again. I saw her grit her teeth as she tossed the ball, and I could feel the effort she was making vibrate through my own body.

But it was a good first serve, just inside the center line and deep, and to my astonishment, Pat followed it up to the net. I'd been about to chip my return short to her forehand, but I faltered, tried to come through on the ball to hit a drive past her backhand, and instead smacked it into the net.

Pat stayed back on her next serve, and we exchanged ground strokes, backhand to backhand. Cautiously, aware of the wind at my back, I waited for a chance at an approach shot. I tried to move in on the ball, taking it high off the bounce to hit it cross-court, but I was overanxious, and it sailed away into the alley.

"Hey!" said Mr. Trask, in an injured tone. "I give my girl a compliment, and she falls apart!"

Nobody laughed. Pat had walked up to the net to pick up a ball, and she gave me an odd, searching look, hard and almost unfriendly. I glanced over at Mom and Dad, seeing their tense expectant faces. *Anything to keep the score from being so lopsided this time,* my mother had said.

And I realized what Pat's look meant, as clearly as if she'd spoken the words aloud. *Are you*

*letting up on me, Dulcie? Because if you are, don't.
Don't you dare!*

I hadn't meant to, but . . . two careless errors in a row, when I'd been at the top of my game only a few minutes before? Maybe it was true. Maybe I'd decided unconsciously to let this game go, or at least not to fight Pat too hard for it. If she won her serve, and then I won mine, the set would be over; but at least the score would be 6–3.

Thirty–love. Pat served well again, and again came up to the net. I didn't try for a passing shot. Instead I hit the ball straight at her, at waist level, as hard as I could. For an instant I thought of my doubles partner, Sam, back there at the beginning of the summer, and how in a way everything had started with him. . . .

Pat jerked her racket across her body in self-defense, and the ball banged off it harmlessly into the net.

"Hey!" she protested. "Unnecessary roughness." But she stood smiling at me for a moment—her best smile, open and generous, that transforms her face.

I smiled back. "Just putting you in your place," I said.

And she didn't try coming to the net again. On the next point, I got off my good old topspin return of service deep into the backhand corner, the one shot remaining from my old tennis days. It rocked Pat back on her heels, and she mis-hit it into the net.

At 30–all, we had another backcourt rally. This time I made myself wait until I had a good chance at a winner, keeping my drives flat and low so the wind couldn't tamper with them, trying to maneuver Pat out of position. At last she hit a forehand drive that fell a little short—you could see she was getting exhausted, hitting into that miserable wind—and I was able to put the ball away down the line before she could reverse direction and get to it.

Thirty–forty, and set point. I was determined to end it then and there. I had the feeling that if the score went on to deuce, it would all be just too much for Pat; maybe too much for both of us. "Advantage, Miss Kane . . ." I remembered Amy's imaginary tournament and smiled to myself a little sadly.

Pat missed her first serve, and the second barely cleared the net. The wind pushed the ball sideways, almost out into the alley, but it just caught the line. By the time I'd finished scrambling for it, I was way out of position, practically up at the net pole. My return hadn't gone very deep, and Pat had the whole court open for her shot; but either she hit it too cautiously or she was just tired. Anyway, the ball didn't have much pace, and as it came over the net the wind caught it and held it a moment before it bounced. The effect was a perfectly placed drop shot into my backhand service court.

I don't know how I got to the ball, or what I thought I was going to do with it when I got there.

I just dove at it with my racket outstretched, and the ball rebounded weakly off the strings. It literally climbed the net, wavered back and forth along the tape, and then, after what seemed a lifetime, fell . . . over onto Pat's side.

Game, set, and match—the match that Mrs. Trask had wanted and had taken such care to arrange. I didn't feel any sense of triumph, but neither could I feel regret. As I got to my feet and brushed myself off, I thought only: Well, that's that. I did what I had to do, and now it's over.

Pat shook my hand across the net and gave me a brief hug. I couldn't see her face.

Mr. Trask called, "You had the angels with you on that one, Dulcie!"

Pat said, "Yes, but it was Dulcie who landed on her chin," and everybody laughed. Together we walked over to the bench.

Amy said, "You were both terrific!" and Mom handed Pat her sweater and asked where was mine—I hadn't brought one—and all of a sudden everyone was being very casual about the whole thing. Dad said it was too bad about the wind, it was enough to throw anybody's game off—made you realize what an important shot the lob was. . . .

"I could have lobbed all afternoon," Pat interrupted, speaking in a firm, clear voice, "and I still wouldn't have been able to beat Dulcie."

Everyone stopped talking and looked at her,

and I saw Johnny straighten up with a kind of light in his eyes.

"Of course it would have been nice to get the ball *past* her once in a while," Pat conceded, frowning down at the ground. Then she looked at me and laughed and flung out her arms in an exuberant un-Pat-like gesture.

"Mom! Dad! Everybody!" She whirled around. "Do you realize what we have here? Do you have any idea how good she's going to be? Oh, *Dulcie!* I'm so excited for you!"

She gave me another hug, a big one this time. I knew in that moment Pat had forgotten about losing, forgotten about how she looked, what other people were thinking, all of it. She was thinking only of me. Suddenly I felt like crying.

"Good girl," I heard Mrs. Trask murmur; and I knew which one of us she meant.

And now everyone was talking at once. My parents were asking Mrs. Trask all kinds of questions, and she was explaining about setting up a regular practice schedule for me after school and finding a partner. Which was the best of the local indoor courts? No, she didn't intend to enter me in a tournament for another year or so, she wanted to be sure I was ready. As for rackets—metal perhaps, or maybe one of the new laminated types. . . . I wanted to listen, but Amy had come up and grabbed my arm and was bubbling away enthusiastically in my ear.

"Hey, you realize you never even had to ask what the score was?" When I looked blank, she explained, "Well, remember how we always used to lose track of the points, and even the games, and we'd stop and argue and sometimes have to start all over again? But today . . ."

I was watching Pat and Johnny, who were standing over to one side, laughing about something. Pat wasn't even bothering to keep the good side of her face turned toward him. Mom would say it was woman's intuition, a phrase Pat hated, but wouldn't it be great if Pat and Johnny actually—

"Dulcie?" I became aware that Amy had taken a step back and was staring at me intently. "You know something? You've changed."

"I have?"

She nodded, looking solemn. "The way you were playing today. . . . Oh, I know your tennis is lots better, your strokes and all, but I don't mean that. I mean the way you went after every single point, even when you didn't need it. Like you were winning, anyway . . ."

She broke off a little uncomfortably, glancing over at Pat.

"Well, I mean, you'd probably slaughter me, for instance, if we were ever playing together." Amy gave me an uncertain look.

I nodded. "I probably would," I said and grinned at her.

"You see—that's what I mean." Then her eyes widened. She said in a awed voice, "You know what it is? It's the *killer instinct*! That's what they all have to have, all the top athletes, and tennis players especially. I read this whole article about it, it was called "Going for the Jugular"—that means the jugular vein—and it said—"

"Now, now." Mr. Trask came up behind us and patted our shoulders. "Dulcie may be a tiger on the tennis court, but she's just a sweet little girl the rest of the time. Don't let her scare you, Amy."

Amy laughed, but I looked at him thoughtfully. And I found myself wondering about my father, and whether his present enthusiasm would survive the years ahead, and the kind of life I knew now I wanted for myself.

Mr. Trask glanced around impatiently. "Well, who's ready for some mixed doubles? How about it, Amy, let's us take on Mr. and Mrs. Kane, okay? Come on, Norman," he called to my father. "We've been sitting around long enough in this wind." And he hustled Amy onto the court.

I sat down on the bench next to Mrs. Trask, who gave me what I recognized by now as a professional appraisal: was I tired, how did I feel about the way I'd played, did I know what things I had to work on? But before she could say anything, my mother looked up from tying a shoelace and said, "Now, Dulcie, I don't want you to worry about a thing. We'll have to work out some details, but everything will be taken care of, I promise you."

I looked puzzled.

"Housework," she explained. "Cooking. That sort of thing. Obviously you can't play tennis and be bothered with all those old chores."

"But—"

"And if Pat's going to be working out with you several days a week, well . . ." She shrugged. "I guess I'm it."

"Pat is? As my practice partner?" I looked from Mom to Mrs. Trask, and said a little wildly, "But Mom—your job—I don't want you to have to give up your job just because of me. . . ."

"Oh, I've been pretty fed up with Dr. Hebert lately, and anyhow I can always work part-time if I want to. But who knows"—she put on her martyr's look—"I might even get to enjoy loafing around the house all day. Well, for heaven's sake, Dulcie, look at all the things you've been getting done in just a few hours. I certainly ought to be able to manage the house without killing myself. Besides, I've always wanted to learn how to make apple strudel, and they say it takes *hours*."

She walked briskly onto the court to join my father.

I stared after her doubtfully, and then burst out laughing. "I bet I still wind up washing the dishes," I said.

Mrs. Trask smiled. "Maybe not, Dulcie. In fact, you may find there's almost too much pressure on you at home from now on—everybody expecting you to think of nothing but tennis all day long." She sighed. "I guess I'll just have to rely on your own common sense. After all, it's brought you this far."

I saw her glance out at the players warming up on the court, at the bright yellow balls flying back and forth across the net; and I had a moment's pang for her, that she should be sitting here on the sidelines.

"By the way," she said, turning back to me, "nothing's been settled about Pat—about having her play with you, that is. It was your parents' idea, and I think it's a good one. But, of course, you'll have to see how Pat feels about it."

I looked around for Pat, but she and Johnny had left the court and were walking slowly across the sunny field, the white skirt of Pat's tennis dress whipping in the wind.

Mrs. Trask said, "I think she'll do it. Her own game can't help improving in the process, and, of course, I can give her some pointers from time to time. But"—she looked at me severely—"one thing must be clearly understood, Dulcie: you are my pupil, not Pat. Although I don't think we'll have any trouble about that. Not after today."

I could feel her studying me from behind the big dark glasses. Her voice softened as she said, "It's all right, Dulcie, isn't it?"

I nodded. After a moment I reached for my mother's sweater, which she'd tossed down on the bench, and drew it around me—more for comfort than for warmth. I felt suddenly cold and scared and lonely, thinking of all that lay ahead. But the moment passed; I settled back and prepared to watch the doubles.

It was Eric as usual who had the last word. On the way home in the car, he said, "If Dulcie gets to be a tennis player, then I get to have a dog."

He wasn't asking us, he was telling us.

"I know the one I want," he went on. "It's a she, and it has gold hair, and it likes to run around in circles. I'm going to call it Chris. You know, like that tennis player on TV—the pretty one."

"Oh, Eric!"

Pat's eyes met mine, and we both began to laugh.

epilogue

WE WENT to Forest Hills again last fall, on another
blue September day, but everything else had changed.
Sitting in the stadium, you could still see a few grass
courts in the distance, but the tournament surface
was gray, a slow gray clay; and the European clay-
court players dominated the play with their long,
patient, baseline rallies. I have a feeling I'll be working hard on ground strokes again this winter—though
as Pat pointed out, the women's pro circuit uses a
fairly fast surface, and there are cement courts in
California (I may be going out to California later this
year) and grass in Australia. . . . Johnny leaned past
Pat to wink at me, and said, "And of course there's
always Wimbledon, Dulcie." Which was just what I
was thinking myself.

Eric decided to name his dog Martina instead of Chris, after seeing Martina Navratilova play a match on television. He liked the way she bounced around at the net—"just like a puppy," he said. He still prefers watching tennis on TV, where you can see the players close up.

About the Game of Tennis

Points within a game are scored as follows: love (or 0), 15, 30, 40, game, with the server's score always given first. A score of 30–15, for instance, means that the server has won two points and the receiver one. If the score goes to 40–40—called *deuce*—a player must win two successive points to win the game. The player winning the first point after deuce has the *advantage,* or "ad"; if he loses the next point, the score reverts to deuce.

The winner of a *set* is the player who first wins

six games by a margin of at least two games over his opponent. Thus a game score of 6–5 does not end a set. If the leading player wins the next game, the set is his at 7–5; if, on the other hand, the score is tied at 6–all, modern practice is to play a tie-breaker, usually a 9- or 12-point exchange scored in conventional consecutive numbers.

SOME TENNIS TERMS

Baseline. The back line of the court.

Service line. The line parallel to the baseline which marks the boundary of the service court.

Alley. The extra strip along the sides of the singles court, used only in doubles play.

Deuce court. The right-hand side of the court.

Advantage court. The left-hand side of the court.

Service ace. An unreturnable serve.

Service break. A game won by the receiver.

Fault. A serve that misses. If the server misses both serves he has *double faulted* and has lost the point.

Rally. A prolonged exchange of shots; also practice hitting or warming up before a game.

Volley. A shot hit before the ball bounces.

Lob. A stroke that lifts the ball high in the air.

Cross-court shot. A stroke that angles the ball diagonally across the court.

Down-the-line-shot. A stroke that sends the ball parallel and close to a sideline.

Approach shot. A hard, deep drive enabling a player to come to the net for his opponent's return.

Passing shot. A shot hit beyond the reach of a player at the net.

Drop shot. A ball hit short, so that it just drops over the net.

Flat shot. A stroke hit with little or no spin.

Topspin. A spin put on the ball by stroking up and over it with the racket, increasing its forward rotation.